RUINS
OF THE FALL

I0555998

BOOK TWO
THE REMNANTS TRILOGY

NICHOLAS ERIK

Published by Watchfire Press.

This book is a work of fiction. Similarities to actual events, places, persons or other entities are coincidental.

Watchfire Press
www.watchfirepress.com
www.nicholaserik.com

Cover design by Kerry Hynds
www.hyndsstudio.com

Ruins of the Fall/Nicholas Erik. – 1st ed.
Print ISBN: 978-1-940708-77-5
e-ISBN: 978-1-940708-86-7

FROZEN WASTES

THE
GRAY DESERT

THE
NEW ALLIED STATES

UNKNOWN

NORTH AMERICAN CIRCLE c. 2051

ASHES OF THE FALL RECAP

ASHES OF THE Fall begins in March 2048 on North American Circle Anniversary Day. Con man Luke Stokes has traveled to New Manhattan from his home in the Western Stronghold because of a cryptic message from his genius brother, who he hasn't seen in fifteen years: *I need to see you by tomorrow. Come to 1611 Park Boulevard. Here's something to help you. You'll have to figure your way through customs on your own, though. I have a project that requires your skills. – Matt*

Chancellor Tanner, leader of the Circle, recaps past events during the anniversary address: the world flooded in 2025, sending an influx of refugees into the then United States. Through a series of engineering programs—raising the coastlines—the United States managed to survive the floods. But the expense and strain plunged the existing country into disarray.

In 2026, after a series of so-called terrorist attacks in the South perpetrated by religious fanatic Damien Ford, a single group—the Circle—seized power. Stability required a number of concessions: the Religious Suppression Act of 2026, which outlawed the open practice of any religion, and the Computing Standardization Act of 2027, which brought all technological development under control of the Circle.

During NAC Anniversary Day, a 9.3 magnitude earthquake along the Cascadian fault line rocks the Northwest. A volcanic eruption at the Yellowstone volcano showers much of the West in ash.

Luke finds his brother murdered in his apartment. Special Committee Agents are already en-route. To survive, he takes his brother's HoloBand—a small microchip implanted at the base of his neck, which connects to one's neural wiring. A HoloBand identifies a person, allows them to make financial transactions, and enables access to the HoloNet, a brain-extension network of information. Thus, Luke "becomes" Matt Stokes.

Luke is taken to the Origin Point, a gleaming capital at the center of Manhattan. He meets with none other than Chancellor Tanner, who is paranoid and locked in his ivory tower, having not made a public appearance for years. Tanner is dying, and is curious about the progress of a project called HIVE, which he says will save humanity. Luke learns that his brother was a member of the Inner Circle—a group of twelve decision makers—and worked closely with Tanner. Matt was taken when he was fourteen, and placed in a special Circle run program called Gifted Minds, for genius children.

After following a trail of leads, Luke finds that all but one of the engineers involved with the HIVE project have been murdered. From the surviving engineer, he receives a box with an antiquated 2.5" SSD drive labeled "The Antidote," a beta version of HIVE running on a not-yet-released HoloBand 6.0, and a two-page suicide note from Matt. Luke gives Tanner the HIVE beta, which Tanner tells him is incredible and will save the world.

Afterward, Luke meets with Olivia Redmond, who claims to be helping Matt enact his plan from the grave. But Olivia instead shoots Luke, then turns him in. Luke is sentenced to death and sent to the newly opened Other-lands—the wreckage of the South is now a place to send those with criminal tendencies, separating them from "polite" society.

On the Hyperloop, he meets Kid Vegas—son of the infamous Damien Ford. They're saved by Director Black-stone, head of the Otherlands, who is working with Oliv-ia Redmond. Blackstone wants to quietly remove Tanner from power, and needs HIVE to do so.

Luke, not trusting anyone, escapes the first chance he gets, living in an abandoned FEMA camp and barter-ing with a mysterious group of nomads called the Rem-nants. But six months later, Kid Vegas hauls him back to the Otherlands. Luke is sent after the remaining HIVE drives—there are three total, of which two are still miss-ing. He retrieves one drive, and begins looking for the other.

But then Luke discovers the truth about HIVE from an old associate of Matt's: it's a virtual reality construct that people can jack into and escape reality (HIVE: Ho-loBand Interactive Virtual Existence). Whoever controls this technology will be able to offer a downtrodden popu-lace an antidote to a gritty, tiresome world. Matt designed HIVE as a mutually assured destruction plan, distributing sections of the source code to each of the factions. Even if the source code was assembled, it requires his Holo-Band in order to run as a final fail-safe.

Luke finds his brother's secret research facility deep in the middle of the Otherlands. There he discovers Matt "alive"—existing as an artificial intelligence construct downloaded to a computer mainframe. This demonstrates the true power of HIVE and the technology behind it: the code is powerful enough to store and even potentially create human consciousness. However, before Luke can decide what to do with HIVE, he is captured by Kid Vegas and taken to a hidden server farm.

It is then revealed that Olivia Redmond, Kid Vegas—who were part of Gifted Minds—and Director Blackstone, who ran Gifted Minds, have been using Luke to retrace Matt's steps and secretly track down the HIVE source. Olivia killed Matt, and created a series of clues for Luke to follow—a con artist move. They also needed him invested in Matt's supposed "plan"—his "suicide" note was a forgery orchestrated by Blackstone, talking about "great sacrifice"—because Luke is the only one who could run Matt's HoloBand—the literal key to making HIVE function.

Olivia Redmond kills Tanner—revealed that Tanner consciousness was kept alive via the HIVE beta. Director Blackstone seizes control of the Circle.

With the source code fully-assembled, Luke is jacked into HIVE, along with Evelyn Vera and Carina Alonso, where he remains for three years in blissful stasis. He's in a relationship with Evelyn, and they have a nice, big dog named Ramses.

At the end of the book, Jana Rose, a member of the Remnants, breaks Luke out of HIVE. She tells him there's an all-out factional war between the Lionhearted, Circle, Ashes of the Fall and Remnants. And they need Luke Stokes to end it.

1 | ALL THAT REMAINS

As Jana Rose drags me into the fire-scorched streets of New Manhattan, my eyes tear up from the smoky haze. Through the blur, I recognize my brother's apartment building. Which is when I realize that I was inside the Gifted Minds research facility down the street. It makes sense that Chancellor Tanner would locate the server farm here. The security infrastructure was already in place—and besides, there's a full circle synchronicity about it that even I can appreciate.

This is where Matt's new life began.

And now I'm experiencing a similar revival.

Still, even in my slightly confused state, it strikes me as an audacious *fuck you* from the now-deceased Tanner. The server farm was right under my brother's nose the entire time and he simply had no idea. Like Tanner was daring him to find it, and Matt came up short.

Then again, Tanner had no idea about all the looping contingencies built-in to HIVE, so I guess they were both a little behind the curve.

"Come on, Luke," Jana says, smoke cloaking her face. "We only have a couple minutes."

I just woke up from a three-year sleep, so I'm not

moving too fast. Every time I move my head, image artifacts streak through my vision. A large dog, fragments of an idyllic life that was never real. I shake my head, trying to get rid of the cobwebs.

Instead, it just makes everything worse.

Jana, fed up with waiting, yanks my arm hard enough that it hurts. "Our people are *dying*, Luke. They didn't save you to daydream."

A rocket bursts into one of the high-rises down the street. Was it Matt's old apartment? Where Olivia Redmond shot him in the head only moments before I arrived? It's impossible to tell in the swirling chaos. Glass and twisted metal stream down as panicked residents shriek. One thing's for sure: the people of New Manhattan aren't used to this sort of disturbance.

Jana pushes me toward a car and shoves me inside. It's not an automatic, which means she has to drive it. Before I can ask her if she's up to it, she floors the accelerator so fast that my head whips back into the seat. The two-door sedan shoots through the debris and heavy ash.

"What about your people?"

"The Hyperloop station," Jana says. "Half an hour. They know the drill."

"What happens if they're late?"

Her expression tells me all I need to know.

"Might want to buckle up," Jana says. As if on cue, a vehicle pulls in behind us, clinging to our tail. I recognize the driver's uniform—Special Committee. Good to see there's been a lot of progress in the past three years.

"The secret police are up our ass," I say, squinting in the rearview only to catch sight of a familiar face. No—it couldn't be. I can't trust my senses right now, but I swear that it's the same bastard who jacked me into HIVE.

The man leans half his body out the window, his perfect side part barely moving in the stiff breeze.

"You see this asshole?" I say.

"How can I not see him?"

"You remember him?"

"Should I?"

I think *yeah*, because I'm pretty sure this guy was there when Jana was lying in the middle of the road and I saved her from being shot like a dog. But then again, she wasn't in the clearest mental state at the time.

A bullet explodes from the barrel of his rifle, shattering our back windshield. It lodges itself in the padded headrest, only two inches below Jana's exposed head.

"It's Kid Vegas," I say, no longer doubting myself. Not many men who can make that shot. "You gotta swerve."

"I'm trying," Jana says. She whips the wheel, taking the car down a narrow alley. The side mirrors are immediately ripped off as we scrape against the walls. The pursuing sedan follows us without slowing down. Kid is forced back inside the vehicle. In the rearview, I see him urging his driver to speed up.

The expressionless agent floors it, sending the car's front fender hurtling into our backside. We both rocket out of the narrow street, headed straight for a jewelry store's window display.

At the last minute, with our tires already touching the sidewalk, Jana brakes and cuts the wheel almost a full hundred eighty degrees. Our sedan launches into a tailspin, colliding against the glass with a thunderous *crack*. Kid's vehicle, still going almost full speed, rushes past and slams against the back wall.

"We gotta go," Jana says. She unhooks her seatbelt with the casualness of someone about to head to the movies. "The station's only a couple miles from here."

"How long we got?"

"Not long enough to sit here and ask questions." Jana's door is already open.

I look into the ruined store, trying to see if Kid is still alive. There's no movement from the smoking sedan. I can't see how he survived. It gives me a small sense of satisfaction, knowing that the person who stole three years of my life—conned me out of them—is six feet under. But then a series of hallucinations burst across my vision, and I'm brought back to the reality of my other problems.

A dog's shrill, incessant bark pounds in my ears.

"You hear that?"

"It's the engine," Jana says. "We gotta go, Luke."

"No, it's a dog."

She gives me a funny look, her tattoo scrunching up around the edges of her eyes. "There's no dog, Luke?"

Woof. Woof. I hold me hand out, as if to say *enough*, but it won't stop. "Don't tell me there's no dog."

"You don't look so good."

"I'm fine," I say. My ribs ache from the strap digging into my chest. "Just give me a hand, all right?"

Jana helps me undo my seatbelt. It takes a couple tries to open my ruined door, but eventually I manage to stumble out on to the sidewalk. The neighborhood's residents have woken up and are looking down from their apartments. But everyone is too afraid to come down for a closer inspection.

And so Jana and I run off into the empty night, toward the station.

*

I STARE OUT the Hyperloop's windows, at the barren soil racing past. The steel handcuffs feel cool against my wrists. A light frost covers the ground outside. The damaged Hyperloop moves slow enough that I can get a glimpse of the landscape. Footsteps patter against the capsule's metal floor, but I don't turn. Even though there's little to see, I'm fascinated by reality.

After all, three years have passed in what seems like nothing more than a single, halting breath.

From nowhere, an image of a big dog lying on the grass flashes across my field of vision. I recoil from the window, heart racing.

"Ramses?" I say. But there's no dog. Only the infinite emptiness of the open plains.

"Hey," Jana says, shaking my arm. "*Hey.*"

I turn to her with a half-sneer to mask my fear. "I'm thinking. You might recognize it if you ever did it." Adjusting to reality is tough, especially after you've spent the last three years in utopia. I catch myself wishing, in the recesses of my subconscious, that I could go back. Especially since the world of HIVE seems to be bleeding into the actual world anyway.

"We didn't bust you out to think," she says. Her green eyes flash in the dim light as the train car rattles forward. I can see that she's taken a gunshot to the arm. Or maybe it's from a blade. Either way, the cost of my freedom has indeed been high.

Blood drips down her torn sleeve, but she barely notices.

"You're bleeding," I say, pointing at her injured arm. Well, as best I can—since my hands are shackled, I can't raise them to quite the right height. "So you broke me out because you wanted me for your own prison?"

That's not it, of course. I'm valuable: I'm what makes the entire HoloBand Interactive Virtual Existence run. As the only one who can use my brother's HoloBand—the key to the entire system—I might be the single most valuable person alive.

Nathaniel Blackstone's gonna be pissed when he hears about this.

"Just a flesh wound," Jana says, her fingertips lightly brushing over the torn skin. The Rems must not feel pain the same way as a normal human. Out on the middle of the highway in The Lost Plains, I remember she was three-quarters-dead, and still stronger than me. Whatever the Remnants are, it's a heartier stock than the rest of us.

So I can actually take her at her word, that it's just a flesh wound.

"So you broke me out for my good looks," I say. "Since it wasn't for my brilliance."

"We have a plan."

Her punkish, dark black hair barely moves when she shrugs. Jana flashes a grim smile that shows a row of strong, white teeth. Coupled with the tattoo running along the right side of her face—an elaborate tangle of beautifully inked vines and flowers—the expression makes her look totally insane.

But then, she'd have to be, to plunge into the heart of New Manhattan and snatch me directly from the Circle's jaws.

"You know the Circle is gonna come after you with everything they got." Must be Stockholm Syndrome. But

I'm thinking my old captors—Blackstone, Olivia and whoever else heads up the Circle these days—might be preferable to my new ones.

Jana just replies, "It's like I told you near the servers."

My mind flashes back to the white-washed, antiseptic room filled with pods, streaked in blood and soot because of the raid. The signs of war somehow made the scene less surreal. Probably would've shit myself if I'd seen endless rows of humans suspended in virtual reality stasis. But most of the pods had already been destroyed by the time I'd woken up.

High costs indeed.

"The world needs a hero," I say, dredging up Jana's words from a sea of cluttered thoughts. I also manage to recall some other ominous snippets of our terse conversation.

All-out war.

This is only the beginning.

I swallow hard when I recall the last directive: *I'm the only one who can end it.*

As if reading my mind, Jana says, "You're the only one who can end it."

I jump slightly in my seat. The cuffs rattle. She touches my arm, not gently, but more like how you'd control an overly skittish dog. I brace myself against the capsule's glass window, breathing heavily.

Then I laugh.

"You find this funny?"

"Not really," I say. But it's dawned on me—the reason for HIVE. The *necessity* for it. We are all afraid of life's vastness. The empty plains on which we can make our mark. Life is not short. It is excruciatingly long, and we need a way to burn our time, distract us from the immensity and absurdity of our existence.

This is particularly true when our real existence is painful.

We are all trying to distract ourselves from the misery. Before, we succeeded with more mundane methods. Silly stories, computer games with photo-realistic graphics. But now, we don't need to live vicariously at all.

Technology, in its omnipresent march onwards, has eradicated yet another middleman. With HIVE, we can *live* the way we always wanted: briefly, gloriously, and unconsciously.

"Why'd you laugh, then?" Jana says.

"I think reality is vastly overrated," I say. "Give me HIVE any day."

"You might get your wish."

My blood chills, and I turn. Her green eyes stare at the front of the small Hyperloop capsule hurtling toward—where, I don't know.

"I don't like where this is going," I say.

"A lot of people are mad at you, Luke."

I haven't found myself wishing that the Lionhearted ruled the world often, but right now might be one of those few times. The Biblical notion of turning the other cheek and forgiving those who have thrown stones is comforting.

Unfortunately, it is not reality. I fucked the Remnants over, stole the slice of HIVE source code that my brother gave them for safekeeping. The one bargaining chip that they had, keeping them from destruction.

Didn't matter if my intentions were to fix things. Plans don't work out the way they should, especially when you're being had. Kid, Olivia and Blackstone played me, strung me along, and then pounced once I had put together most of the pieces. I thought I was helping my brother save the world.

But really, I was just passing the baton of power from Chancellor Tanner to Director Blackstone.

You're only ever judged on results. And my results are shit.

"So, with HIVE, is Blackstone—"

"Chancellor, yeah," Jana says. "I told you, Luke. Three fucking years happened." Her voice sizzles with annoyance, but somewhere, in the layers of hurt, I sense sympathy. She doesn't think whatever the Rems have planned for me is the correct play.

I wish she would tell me. Being unceremoniously cuffed without explanation tends to get the mind conjuring up a host of nasty scenarios.

I look down where she's rolling a small plastic case between her fingers. It's no larger than a tube of lipstick, and Jana doesn't strike me as prim. Although her heart shaped face and brilliant eyes make her pretty—elegant in the same way a German Shepherd is.

"What's that?"

"Your HoloBand," Jana says. "You look surprised."

"Surprised you shot straight with me? Yeah, I guess." I remember, when I first woke up, the slight prick at the back of my neck. She must've removed it right then. Just as well. It tracks my location when it's implanted, amongst a host of other frightening abilities that I'm not sure qualify as advancements. Least of all its capability of being the lynchpin for a massive interconnected virtual reality network.

"With this, you're still valuable," Jana says, rolling the case around in her palm. "Without it…"

A screen at the capsule's front flickers on, snatching everyone's attention. The familiar face of the Circle's propaganda network—the silver-haired newscaster I affectionately call Old Silver Fox—clears his throat before an urgent "news" announcement.

"This should be good," I say. Although I'm loath to admit it, I'm curious if the tenor of the Circle's media relations has changed. I have my doubts that Nathaniel Blackstone is a more benevolent dictator than his murdered predecessor, despite Blackstone's wizened visage.

Jana raises a finger to her lips. There's a certain irony, that the Remnants actually care what this guy has to say. But I soon see why.

"HIVE is currently experiencing scheduled downtime for a massive firmware upgrade," Old Silver Fox begins with gravitas, "but functionality will be restored by the end of the week. Citizens are encouraged to rely on the legacy HoloNet infrastructure. A full statement from our Secretary of Technology, Kid Vegas, can be found at our HoloNet address."

So the bastard survived—or at least, that's the party line for now. Should've expected that.

"Poor citizens," I say, giving a sideways glance to Jana, "You're making them use the shitty old HoloNet, now? The porn on that is barely interactive."

"Shut up," she says.

"And now, breaking and exciting news from our leader," Old Silver Fox says, although he hardly looks excited. "Chancellor Blackstone, in a statement exclusive to CMN, has announced a peace accord with the Lionhearted and Ashes of the Fall. This will mark the end of a three-year conflict. For Circle Media & News, I'm—"

Someone at the front of the capsule tosses their boot at the screen, shattering it. The sound dies with a hissing groan. The small car erupts into a blitz of noise as the Remnants fight amongst each other. I don't say anything, but I do smile somewhat smugly to myself.

A shot to the ribs breaks me out of my silent victory.

"What're you so happy about?" Jana says. "This means we don't need you."

"Or maybe you need me more than ever."

"I doubt that," she yells above the fray, then quickly rises, leaving me alone. As the noise swirls around me, I stare at the empty plains. In the distance, I swear I see a fire. I wonder who lives out there, in the wreckage. Is it a battle? A group of wanderers, trying to survive?

Jana's final words ring in my ears. What is Blackstone's end game—what does this peace treaty afford him that war could not? The fact that I can't even fathom an answer makes me shiver.

I crane my neck to peer at the fire, but the horizon is swallowed up by the night.

Even a slow Hyperloop is too fast for the speed of life.

2 | AMBUSH

JANA'S RIGHT: I need to make myself useful. Maybe the Circle's bluffing, but if they can get HIVE back online without me, that means my stock drops significantly. And it seems unlikely that Blackstone's looking to split the power dynamic four ways.

Lots of complications to my life already, and I've only been awake for a couple hours.

But there's at least one I'm not expecting. Because when I see Carina Alonso and Evelyn Vera for the first time in three years—at least *really* see them, for real—I have to stop. They're standing out on the Hyperloop platform, near what used to be the entrance to the Otherlands.

"You're holding the line up," the Remnant guard behind me says. He pushes be forward and I almost stumble and fall. "Let's go, Sleeping Beauty."

"Didn't take you for someone who could read," I say.

"Just fucking move it." This time, when he puts his hands on me, I fly face-first into the dust. The cuffs scrape against the ground. The platform opened only three years ago, but it's already lost quite a bit of its luster. The Circle's insignia—a circle with a small gap at the top, where a small star resides—has already faded. In another few years, the paint will be gone.

The platform is abandoned, and the tube enclosing the Hyperloop is scorched by flame and marred by graffiti. I see that the rattles and shakes were caused by the dead weight at the end—at least ten capsules which sit askew, roofs ripped to shreds.

The tube wobbles and shakes as the last passengers disembark. The machine seems unsure whether it can continue operating. Judging from the state of affairs, the Circle's grand plan of separating criminals from the rest of society didn't go as planned.

"Get up." The guard hauls me up by the shoulder. "Enough sightseeing."

I shake him off and walk over to Evelyn and Carina.

"So you're alive," I say, because nothing else comes to mind. They share a glance after looking at my cuffs. But there's no chance for either of them to comment before we're herded toward the broken turnstiles at the end of the platform. There's a certain circular nature to all of this—since I met Carina at similar gates in New Manhattan—but the situation is far different.

No one mans the booths to scan our HoloBands. Here, we just step over the rusted metal and walk outside to the abandoned road. In the distance, I can see the outline of Atlanta. The towering skyline is just as I remember it—no worse, no better. Slick, as president of the Ashes of the Fall, hasn't had time to initiate a public works program.

"If I'd have known we were visiting Slick, I would've made cookies," I say once we stop. There's no sign of life around for miles. Neither Carina nor Evelyn smile. Not getting a response gnaws at me more than I'd like to admit. "Maybe one of you—"

"Cut the shit, Luke," Jana says, appearing from behind me. "We're not going to Atlanta."

"Glad you're still here," I say, shaking the cuffs as she moves in front of me. "I think you forgot something."

Jana smirks, but doesn't respond.

"She's trading you," Evelyn says. "Idea was, the world would go to shit if HIVE went down. Then the Remnants would give back the HoloBand and you, restore order, and everyone would stop hunting them."

"Be quiet," Jana says.

"Maybe you should speak to your lackeys a little softer," Evelyn says.

Well, at least I know why Evelyn and Carina aren't cuffed. They just aren't worth that much as trade bait.

Dirt bikes hum in the open distance, maybe five minutes away. The Remnant guards stand at attention, their breaths shortening. Nerve-wracking, being so close to the Ashes of the Fall.

Imagine if you're cuffed and weaponless. I manage to keep my cool, though.

"Was it your idea," I say to Jana, who's scanning the horizon for threats.

She just doesn't turn, just answers, "No."

"That's refreshing."

"It's a dumb plan," she says. "At best, it would've bought us a temporary reprieve. But now, after all that's happened—you're worthless. Like I said."

"I changed the world," I say. "I wouldn't call that worthless."

The growling engines grow louder.

"Ruining the world," Jana says. "Invaluable."

"Can't ruin what's already broken," I say. "Who wanted to cut this deal?"

"Just shut up, Luke."

Easy to say when your ass doesn't depend on sweet-talking your way out of an impossible situation. "Just tell me who it was."

"Vlad."

My breath catches. The leader of the Remnants.

Her father.

"Shit."

"And you haven't even met him," she says. "He's scarier in person." I watch as she brings her rifle scope up to her eye. "These aren't us."

There's a chill to her words, but no fear.

"What do you mean, not us," the guard behind me says, clearly wetting himself. Serves the prick right, throwing me around like a sack of moldy beans. "They're on schedule."

"They were supposed to change the flag from red to green when they were four miles out," Jana says. "It's still red."

The surviving contingent of Remnants—about a hundred strong—clamber for their rifles.

"We gotta move out," Jana says.

"Where?" a soldier calls.

"Just follow me." She starts to run toward a processing facility, maybe three hundred yards from the station platform. Plain concrete. It bears the Circle's official insignia.

It's like a stampede, fear overtaking the group who,

only hours before, undertook a suicide mission to save me. Funny how the mind works. Certain death is acceptable.

Uncertain death is far more frightening.

"Did you see," Carina whispers into my ear as we hurry along the ruined road. She touches the chain around her neck—empty, the cross taken by the Circle. "The people along the Hyperloop. Praying."

"Praying?"

"The fire in the distance."

I nod, but don't speak. Wishful thinking on her part, but I leave her imagination alone. I get the impression she wants to cling to my shirt sleeve. This isn't New Manhattan, and she's never been outside its comparatively kind walls. But she doesn't—three years in the HIVE must've changed the naïve, idealistic young woman I once knew.

I sprint along the pitted concrete, following the Remnants. I consider breaking off in the confusion to toss my lot in with whoever killed our welcoming party. But it strikes me that they're not a friendly bunch either—and if Jana's right, and no one needs me any more, I can only imagine that my fate will not be kind.

When we reach the building, I stop to read the pitted sign over the door.

EXECUTION CHAMBER

Scores lots of points for brevity and clarity, although it lacks lyricism. This must be where I was destined to go when I was sentenced to die. I spot a non-functioning camera in the corner.

And they were gonna broadcast the whole thing. Can't say I miss the old Circle.

Carina and Evelyn have disappeared inside by the time I stop daydreaming.

"Everyone hurry up," Jana calls from the doorway as she ushers the surviving Remnants into the building. "Blackstone's search parties have been a pain in our ass."

Bodies push past, so I stand tight against the wall to avoid getting hit.

"You sure it's safe in here?" I say, eying the sign. Flecks of rust creep at the edges.

"We're not gonna die," Jana says. "At least not from anything in here."

"How comforting."

"The world we live in," Jana says, bringing her rifle up to examine the blackened landscape.

"Should've let me keep sleeping."

"What's the fun in that," Jana says with a grin. Then she reaches into the folds of fabric and flicks me the key to the cuffs. I snag them out of the air.

"You're sure about this?"

"Worthless might've been a little harsh," she says, checking the munition in the rifle. "After all, you caused this shitshow."

"Thanks?"

"That counts as a compliment in these times, Luke," she says, flashing those white teeth again. "You take what you can get."

Don't know if this is a subtle dig at my modus operandi to date, which can best be summarized as *save my own ass*. But there's no time for psychoanalysis. I don't want her to change her mind, so I unlock the cuffs, rub some feeling back into my wrists and then stare her straight in the eyes.

"Why' Blackstone wanna kill you so damn bad?" I say, breathing heavy, my body poorly acclimated to actual physical exertion.

"People always want to destroy what they don't understand," Jana says with a faraway look in her eye. "It's not just Blackstone. It's all of them."

This is a prime opportunity to provide her with an alternative to handing me over. Prove my worth. But nothing comes to mind. Nervous voices filter out from the concrete building.

All I can do is stand by Jana and wait. Maybe solidarity is enough.

I follow her gaze, to the approaching legion of dirt bikes.

"It's gonna take a lot to win over my people," Jana says. She reaches into her waistband. I think she's about to hand me a gun, but it's actually a detonator.

"What are you doing?" I take a step back.

"They're pissed at you, Luke," Jana says. "Your brother, we loved him for giving us a chance in this world. Hope. And you took that all away."

"I was trying to fix things."

"Intentions don't matter much on the plains. You took that HIVE source from our vault, and the world's gotten worse for us. Simple as that." Her finger hovers over the button. "But I think you're right."

"Right about what?"

"You're worth a lot more than you've ever let on."

I don't have time to process whether this development is good or bad, because her finger touches the button and a massive explosion erupts on the horizon, where the dirt bikes were a second before. Jana peers into the darkness with a stoic expression.

"They've pulled this shit before, killing our people and impersonating them," she says. "So I placed contingencies on the bikes."

"Just in case," I say, one eye on the smoking horizon, the other on her. I don't want to be on the wrong side of her. "How can I help?"

"You caused our problems, hero," Jana says, no malice in her voice. Just a world-weariness born of a life on the plains. "And you'll fix them, too. *End* them."

She smiles, but I don't. The emphasis on *end* is all-encompassing, total. Knows no bounds.

Then her eyes flash with a hint of worry.

Before I can react, she takes out a pistol, aims it right at my head, and fires.

3 | TELL ME ABOUT IT

"STOP BEING A little bitch," Jana says, and hands me a handkerchief.

"You shot me!"

"You're welcome."

I touch my throat, where the bullet grazed my neck. It's only a flesh wound, but damn if it doesn't bleed. I glance back where Jana put down the ambush party's sole survivor. One of the explosives didn't trigger, and he thought it would be a good idea to play hero.

That never works out well.

I could've told him that from experience.

She disappears inside the execution chamber turned safe zone. A few rousing words later, and she returns.

"What's the plan," I say.

"We wait."

"That sounds like an awful plan."

"We have no transport," Jana says. "The Hyperloop can't make another run. We're lucky we didn't die on the way down."

Glad that the Remnants risked their most prized bargaining chip and the chief's daughter on a rickety hunk of metal that could self-destruct at any moment. Makes me wonder about their chances of winning this fight. Sign of the times, I guess. Desperate plays suddenly become less risky than the status quo.

"So we wait until Blackstone sends an army?" I gesture toward the horizon, where the half-lit monstrosity of Atlanta looms. "Need I remind you where we are?"

"I know better than you," Jana says with a slight growl. It's the sound of someone telling me to back off, but I'm rusty in the human relations department.

I kick at the dusty gravel and say, "Because your plans have been pretty good so far."

"A lot's changed since you've been sleeping," Jana says. I'm surprised she doesn't take the bait.

"I don't see much."

"That's the problem."

"What's the problem?" I say.

"You don't look hard enough." She disappears into the structure, leaving me outside. For the first time, I notice how cold the December frost is. I don't know what the hell the hell all that ash did to the temperature, but I swear it's colder than I remember.

Then again, in HIVE, it barely rained in Seattle. Everything was just a *little* too good to be real.

The aroma of torched metal rides on the gentle breeze. I shiver and turn to go inside. If I'm gonna wait to die, might as well do it beneath a roof

Before I can reach the entry door, an electric-like surge courses through my nerve endings. I drop to one knee, eyes clamped shut. The Space Needle floats into view followed by a huge dog. Evelyn's deep, endless brown eyes stare back at me, mirthful, smiling, waiting for me to kiss her.

I scramble backwards and fall into the dust, trying to blink everything away.

"What the hell?" The sensation is like being drunk, but I haven't taken anything. I try to stumble to my feet, but nothing works right. Instead, I kneel in the ruined soil, the world spinning.

"Don't let Ramses get too far," I hear. "He'll go in the street."

The dog lumbers forward, away from the grass. I feel my body lifted upwards, and I'm running, running, running, chasing down this annoying pet of mine—of *ours*, that belongs to me and Evelyn. I have to go home, get groceries. Make sure I don't get a ticket.

The scene disappears, and I'm back in the dust, sweating like crazy.

I dig my knuckles into the cracked earth until the rough surface tears into my skin. It'd be nice if this was enough to tether me to reality, but it isn't.

This time, I'm taken to a much nastier looking world. This memory doesn't belong to me, though. Almost like I'm looking over someone's shoulder. I recognize the trappings of the Western Stronghold, pre-Yellowstone eruption, pre-quake.

The hand brushes off a sign.

GIFTED MINDS RESEARCH INSTITUTE, WESTERN DIVISION

Then the person whispers, and I hear Matt's voice, "If anything happens, here's the fail-safe."

When the scene evaporates around me, I topple into the dirt. The cold whips against my skin, but I'm not shaking because of the wind chill.

I'm shaking because I'm losing my fucking mind.

A minute later, an hour, a day—hell if I know—I feel

a sharp toed boot in my ribs. I manage to get one of my eyes open, but I don't trust anything. That's what happens when you've been conned—by people, by the system, by a computer program. You develop serious trust issues.

"No," I say, pushing the boot away. "You're not real."

"Like fuck I'm not real," Jana says, and this time she kicks me. The pain is nasty enough that I believe her. I grunt, trying to catch my breath. "The hell are you doing, Luke?"

"Getting a tan," I say. "After all that time in HIVE, I'm pasty as hell."

Her eyes glow with a radioactive annoyance that tells me to get it together. I can't be sure, but I feel that she was less serious three years ago. And more talkative. Although that might just be circumstance.

"You were screaming," Jana says. "You trying to get the wolves on us?"

"Actual wolves?"

"That's not a metaphor, no."

I swing my head around to scan the landscape. We're still alone, with the Hyperloop platform in the distance and the uninviting execution chamber a stone's throw away.

"I'm not going in there."

"No one wants you inside. You sound like you're dying. Worse."

"Help me up," I say, flailing my arm out, still disoriented. She doesn't give me a hand, but I manage to get up anyway. My jeans and thin shirt cling to my skin like I've just been submerged in a pool of water.

After I'm sure that I won't fall over if I try to walk, I lean into Jana's ear. "I saw something."

"I bet you did."

"Listen to me," I say between gritted teeth, the hiss and venom of the words making her eyes stand bolt open. "I mean I saw something that can save our asses. *End* things."

The hum of a motor on the horizon cuts our little détente short. Jana raises her rifle and peers through the scope. Then she nods.

"It's a messenger," she says, walking away. "We stick with the plan."

"What's that," I yell after her.

"You'll be the last to know once we start moving," she says.

I give her the finger as she sprints across the empty plains to greet the coming bike.

HIVE or not, it's the same as it's always been.

I'm on my goddamn own.

4 | BLUFFS

I'M NOT CUFFED again, but that's the only thing I actually like about this new plan. But I'm willing to admit that my reticence is largely due to ignorance. True to her word, Jana has made me the last to know anything.

An hour after the messenger arrived, a fleet of diesel cargo trucks came to pick up the majority of the Remnants. I gave a quick goodbye to Carina and Evelyn, neither of whom seemed particularly put out about our separation.

Then again, their association with me was the reason why they lost three years of their prime years. So I can't blame them. If you date an asshole in your twenties as a woman, you're trading diamonds for empty promises.

But there's no time for guilt, because I'm too busy trying to figure out what the hell is going on. Eight soldiers—along with me and Jana—are headed out in our own truck in a different direction than the others.

The asshole guard who shoved me off the Hyperloop, much to my joy, remains present.

"Where we headed?"

"Children should be seen and not heard," he says. The other Rems get a kick out of this.

"Then why the fuck are you talking?"

I see his broad hands tighten around the stock of his rifle. I brace for a shot to the temple, but apparently my value has increased over the past few hours. The back of the truck goes quiet.

"You got a name?" I say, after a long and awkward silence that's somehow worse than having a discussion.

"Yeah," he says.

"Care to share?" I say. "Since we're working together."

"We ain't working together." He spits on the ground, narrowly missing my boot. "Mirko." The loose rags covering his body don't allow me to see his face or many of his features, but I can tell he's a big bastard.

Mean, too, if his gruff voice is any indication.

"You're a friendly guy." I lean back against the stiff back, my hair touching the canvas. "So I guess Jana wasn't kidding."

"Shuddup," Mirko says.

The truck stops. "We there?" I peek out the small tear in the canvas, but the dark night gives me no clues. "Come on."

I hear Jana say, "Luke, get your ass out here."

Mirko smirks. I can see it in his eyes, the way they squeeze closer together. "Better listen to the boss lady."

"Yeah, I can see why she's not asking for you," I say. When I get up and pass him, I deftly hop over his foot, spying it just in time. Definitely not making any new friends.

The cold hits me like a lash when I jump down from the cargo bed. From what I can tell, we might as well be in the same spot we left. The only difference is that no sign of civilization is present within what looks like a million miles. Can't say I miss the execution chamber, though.

"Nice place," I say.

"What'd you see?" Jana says, kicking rocks with her boot. Despite the cold, she's not bundled up. Her hair moves ever so gently in the harsh winds. Mine is battered all over the place.

"Nothing, since I've been in the backseat with the brain trust—"

"You have a minute before we gotta move on," Jana says. "This goes one of two ways."

"That so?" I walk around the front of the truck, and find that we're at a literal fork in the road. One is an exit, headed off toward Nashville. The other path is unlabeled and continues on and on. I have no idea which is the right way.

"Thirty seconds."

"Jesus, all right." My mind starts spinning. Do I know anything for sure? No. I might be batshit insane. Who knows what prolonged exposure to computer software that, for all intents and purposes, was never meant to be used, can do? It wasn't like Matt performed extensive beta tests on HIVE before Olivia Redmond shot him in the head.

Then again, if I don't offer something, then there is no next play. It all ends here. If I get caught wearing no clothes later on, what does it matter? I'm in the same spot I always was.

"Ten."

"Gifted Minds," I say. "You heard of it?"

"No. Five."

"You skipped a lot of numbers there."

"Last chance," Jana says. Her fingers creep toward the flowing nomadic garb.

"My brother created HIVE and he was part of Gifted Minds and there's a division of the program out West that no one really knows about, far as I can tell, where he put a fail-safe that might be able to save your ass." It all comes out as a long string of words, so rapid that I have to breathe really fast to catch my breath at the end.

Jana doesn't reply. I take it as a good sign that the count doesn't reach zero.

Finally, she says, "Fail-safe?"

"Yeah. Shut the whole thing down," I say. "It's your only real play."

"I'm sure it is."

"Think about it. You said it yourself—everyone's afraid of the Remnants. You're *different*. You'll never be allowed a seat at the table." I swallow hard, the cold air cracking against my dry throat. "They'll hunt you down unless you hunt them first."

There's a long silence, and I think I might've pressed too hard. Then she says, "You ride up front with me."

"Uh, great." I follow her to the truck and climb into the passenger side. "So, you gonna tell me what the first option was?"

"I was going to take you straight to Vlad."

"And what was he going to do?"

Jana adjusts the rearview mirror and glances over before revving the engine. "Since he can't trade you any more, I'd expect he'd make an example out of you."

"And what's option two?"

"You'll find out," Jana says. The door slams, and the engine crackles to life.

My throat is gritty with dust when I swallow.

I've staved off execution this time, but the truth looms, clear as anything.

If I don't escape the Remnants, it's going to be a short-lived respite.

5 | END IT

RIDING IN THE front seat of the truck, I realize that I was wrong.

Not about the hallucination. I have no idea if what I've seen was real. Whether the image was a product of my broken mind, or something Matt coded into the HIVE software as a true fail-safe is impossible to know.

I was wrong about Jana becoming more taciturn. It shouldn't be a surprise. She grew up on the Lost Plains. If that type of experience didn't make her silent, then the last three years of war wouldn't turn her into a mute, either.

Jana rolls from topic to topic as the truck rumbles on, updating me on what I missed over the past three years. To sum up a long and painful series of events in a few words: things got shittier. Blackstone seized power of the Circle in a bloodless coup. Although Tanner was actually executed—I had the privilege of seeing the footage before being placed in HIVE— the official rhetoric was "natural" causes. Blackstone then thoroughly denounced Tanner's regime and the decision to keep HIVE a secret.

Didn't really matter. The Ashes of the Fall and Lionhearted smelled weakness. They were sick of living under the Circle's heel. The Circle might've had HIVE to offer its citizens—a compelling carrot, no doubt—but that didn't stop the conflict.

The Ashes of the Fall tried to encroach on the Eastern Stronghold, the Lionhearted fought dirty with guerilla warfare, and it was generally a big, bloody mess.

The way Jana describes it, the peace treaty from earlier today seems impossible. But Chancellor Blackstone is no fool, and I guess even a momentary disruption in HIVE has left the Circle vulnerable. Better to join forces with your enemies against a weaker bogeyman than to battle at half-strength.

And what better enemy than an actual monster: a group of nomadic, barbarous freaks that the public is already terrified of? Jana doesn't touch on that, and I don't bring it up. The conversation fades for many miles, until she can't handle the silence.

"The messenger said it's true. I don't want to believe it, but I gotta admit it, I guess."

"What's true?" I say.

"No more war." She taps her fingers on the steering wheel. "We're going to live in the New Allied States."

"Catchy."

"They're gonna push us out," Jana says. "Come into the Lost Plains. It's a done deal."

"Not surprising," I say. "Big chunk of real estate."

"Whose side are you on, anyway?"

"I was just saying."

"I know. But it's my home."

There's a hitch in the conversation, and I offer up something real. "I never got to go home. After the ash."

"You lived in the West?"

"Yeah. Buried."

"I'm sorry," Jana says.

"Home is overrated," I say. "Survival is better."

She cracks a smile and steps on the gas. "We might've signed our own death warrant. Bringing everyone together against the people who ruined a good thing."

"Don't want to be the guy who shits on the party," I say. "No one likes that guy."

"We could always give you back," Jana says with a wink. When her green eyes close, it's like a night-light briefly going out. Whatever the hell Damien Ford did down here to create the Remnants, I'm not sure I wanna know.

"Don't even joke about that," I say. "We agreed on option two." Even though I still don't know what option two is, it sounds better than being summarily executed by Vlad.

"You better not be fucking us, Luke," Jana says. "Gas isn't cheap."

"I'm the best chance you got," I say. An unenviable situation for the Remnants: just when they think it couldn't get worse, they *really* need me to be a hero. Not just a hostage held for ransom. "Everyone thinks you're a bunch of—"

I cut myself off, remembering the last time I was blunt with Jana. Three and a half years ago, I even pulled a punch, called her weird when I was gonna say something harsher. She gives me a searing glance, but doesn't respond.

Bump.

Rattle.

The truck picks up speed. Then she says in a quiet voice, "I know damn well how people feel about us."

"Different is scary." I lick the edges of my chapped

lips and look out the window. Still no sign of civilization. Either she's gonna bury me in the middle of the half-frozen landscape, or my proposal worked. "But different can be an advantage. Different is how you end it."

Making sure option two remains the primary plan.

"Don't do that."

"Don't do what?"

"Tell me what I want to hear," Jana says. We swing around a pothole and I collide with the door. She smiles slightly. "It's not good for your health."

"You gotta turn a weakness into a strength," I say, pulling some bullshit chestnut out from an old self-help book I read once.

"Our people are dying. We have less than 10,000 spread out across the Lost Plains."

"The Circle only has, what, a couple million?"

"You like those odds? The rest of humanity, against us?"

"You've survived longer odds out here." I stroke my chin. "You gather your people. All of them."

"I'm not in charge."

"Then get in charge," I say.

"Blackstone and the others have the guns. The drones. Everything," Jana says. "All we have is a bunch of rusty trucks and some dirt bikes that need constant maintenance. We're tired, Luke."

"What was the biggest thing Vlad was getting out of this deal for me?"

"He figured Blackstone would be so damn desperate to plug you back into HIVE that…"

The truck bounces over a pothole, and Jana readjusts the wheel. I wait, but she doesn't seem intent on finishing the thought. A grimace creases her face in the darkness.

"Come on, don't make me beg."

"I'd like to see that, actually." Jana turns down a dirt road. Somehow, the unfinished path is a smoother ride than what remained of the highway. "It's nothing you can give us. Just a dream."

I can't argue with that. But I'm curious, so I say, "Come on. Tell me what one Luke Stokes is worth on the open market."

She gives me a halfhearted smirk and says, "Medicine. Fuel. New vehicles." There's a pause. "A new home."

"Some beachfront property I don't know about?"

"Vlad figured he could trade you for enough cleaner bots and materials to clean up the Western Stronghold," Jana says. "The Gray Desert."

Makes sense. And now, for the first time, I get a good idea of just how much Jana is on my side. To give up even a tiny chance of that deal on what amounts to faith in a lost cause.

"That what they're calling it, now, huh?" I shrug. "Look at it this way."

"This should be good," she says.

"You track down this Gifted Minds institute with me, you get the Gray Desert for *zero* Luke Stokes. Can't beat free."

"You think your presence is worth something?"

"Not too many people can change the world," I say. "Has your old man ever managed that?"

This stumps Jana into silence.

"He's not gonna be happy about this detour," I say. "Can't really backpedal from this."

"I know."

"But option two's not just about me, is it," I say. "It's part of the reason you call him Vlad."

"He killed my mother," Jana says.

I suck in my breath and whistle low. But now I know why Jana is willing to rely on a con man to guide her away.

"You're serious," I say, studying her face. "You're actually serious. Shit."

"Your brother, he wanted to know about the ugly stuff, too."

I don't say anything. We have this in common—our family problems hide in the shadows, forever tormenting us both.

"Wanted to know how we came to be like we are," Jana says. "It's something we don't talk about much. No one wants to talk about what Damien Ford did."

"I understand."

"You can't possibly understand."

Up ahead, I see a light. The conversation will end before I find out what the Remnants are, how they were formed. But Jana is in a talkative mood, and slows down to say, "The government ran experiments. Military projects, you see. Soldiers who wouldn't get tired. Could see in the dark."

"You can see in the dark?"

"A little better than you can," Jana says. "But Damien Ford came through, said we were an abomination. A crime against God. Began destroying the facilities. Scorching the Earth so that there would be no trace of us. Some of us escaped. He killed a lot of people who weren't us in the process."

"Jesus."

"I don't think Jesus can help us," Jana says with a wry grin. "On the plus side, I'm pretty strong. You know that."

I can't tell if she's flirting with me or stating a fact, so I just say, "Yeah, I know."

"On the downside, we don't live too long." She swallows hard. "Max out at around fifty."

"Damn," I say. "Military geneticists dropped the ball on that one."

"It was on purpose, from what we can gather." She shrugs. "You don't want your superhuman army outliving its masters, right?"

"Guess not," I say.

"It's funny," she says, without any semblance of joy or humor, "Damien Ford killed almost all of us. But he also set us free. If not for him, none of us would've escaped. And the Remnants wouldn't exist."

"Well, shit."

"Lot to take in."

"It's been a long day." Fatigue wracks my bones, but my mind remains wide awake. Drinking everything in. Trying to put all the pieces together into some sort of plan that will get me out on the other end alive.

Before I can think, I say, "I know how to end this."

"How?"

"We kill Vlad."

6 | ATLAS

I IMMEDIATELY WANT to snatch the words back from the ether. I'm surprised by how much conviction is behind them. Jana must be, too, because the truck swerves off the road. My head bobs back and forth from the sudden change in terrain before she whips the wheel back on course.

"It's the only way," I say. "You know it's true."

"I actually believe you," Jana says. "Not want to believe you. There's a difference."

"But?"

"It's complicated."

A heavy ball forms in the put of my stomach as I realize that I've just made an actual, unspoken promise.

That I'm going to be the one who kills Vlad.

I feel I need to say something else, but nothing follows. For once, I'm at a complete loss, the only sound the bumpy road and my panicked heart pumping blood into my ears.

"Look, if you're not all in…" I say, feeling the need to hedge my bets a little.

"It needs to happen," Jana finally says. The truck slows down as we approach the lights in the distance. "But I can't say it will."

I change the subject, lest we beat a hasty retreat back toward option one and execution.

"This it," I say, "The Gunpowder Hills?" She said she wasn't taking me to Remnant HQ—but again, trust issues. Not that it'll matter—there's no place within a hundred miles that I can run to for shelter.

"It's a way station," Jana says. "Along the way to the Hills. We're gonna stop for the night. Plan B, remember?"

At least we're still on the same side. On the surface, at least.

"You sure that's a good idea?" I analyze the desolate landscape, imagine Blackstone's drones and foot soldiers already mobilizing to recover their prize. *Me*. "Lot of people want my ass dead. Or alive."

"We'll see anyone three miles before they see us," Jana says. We pull up to the chain link fence. The way station is an old farm. There's no grass in the ruined soil—just dirt—but the barn and two-story early twentieth century house give it away.

Some sections of the fence don't quite match—stretches of six feet tall chain link, interspersed with shorter and vicious looking barbed wire. As the truck pulls up, I swear the headlights glint off a scope in the attic.

Jana rolls down the window and waves her fingers outside. The fence creaks and rattles, our hidden gatekeeper pressing a button from afar.

"Not much of a defense," I say, as we roll slowly on to the property. Jana parks near a dead tree on the far-end of the two-acre spread.

"You touch that fence, you get fried by half a million volts," Jana says.

"That on all the time?"

"It's got a motion sensor," she says. "Conserves energy."

She cuts the engine and gestures for me to get out. I take in the night air—clean and empty. It feels odd, after being in HIVE for so long, where you're bombarded with sensory overload. Out here, there's nothing.

In that way, the unreal is more real. A man isn't used to an environment stripped of everything. I catch a faint whiff of diesel fuel from the truck's exhaust. It makes my heart beat slower.

A man carrying a shotgun over one shoulder, a long-barreled rifle on the other, comes down the house's steps. I see a little boy and girl peeking through the curtains. They disappear when the man whistles.

Jana walks over and gives him a big hug. "Atlas."

"Well, haven't you grown," this man named Atlas says, wrapping her tightly in his sinewy arms. "Didn't expect to see you come my way, Jana Rose."

They release, and Atlas looks at her with an approving nod. Then his gaze turns on me.

His eyes narrow across the plains. The green cuts through the blackness of the night like a laser. The other eight Remnants mill around—some of them sit beneath the tree, others tinker with spare bike parts littered around the farm. Mirko smokes a cigarette off by himself. But it's like Atlas sees none of them.

"So you actually got the son of a bitch," Atlas says. "Luke Stokes, in the flesh."

I walk over, gait measured. Extend my hand.

He looks at it, but doesn't offer his own.

"What they've said on the news, the rumors and all that, I know they ain't true," Atlas says. "But I also know that every lie starts with a grain of truth. So which part is true?"

"Tell me what you want to know."

"You steal the drive from us?"

"I'm a liar and a cheat," I say. "I rip people off to survive." No use bullshitting. "And the first time I tried to do something decent, I fucked all of you pretty bad."

There's a cool pause in the chilly night. He stands bolt still. The receding gray hair makes him look older—fifty or so, which means he's at the end of his time—but the eyes are those of someone fiercely alive, young with the wisdom that only experience can bring.

Funny to imagine that he's ancient in Rem years, since he seems so damn virulent.

Atlas gives my hand a vise-grip squeeze.

"I like him, Jana," he says. "I got your message about the new plan. It's a good one. We can work with this."

Without another word, he gestures toward the house and goes up the stairs. Jana doesn't move for a beat, so I stay with her.

"Wow," she says.

"Interesting guy."

"You really passed," she says.

I don't know what this means, so I shrug.

"I came out here to see if I could trust you."

"So Atlas is your human lie detector?"

"Something like that," she says with a grin. "Let's go inside."

I head up the stairs to the old farmhouse and shake my head. Even if I'm not running a con, I gotta be sharper than this. HIVE has made me slow and weak.

And, out here, where every innocuous moment is a test, even the friendly wolves have a nasty bite.

*

I GUESS I should be happy that I'm winning Jana over to my side.

But I'm paranoid that, at any moment, she could change her mind. Have a change of heart and realize that fighting an army of two million while searching for a hallucinated research facility is stupid.

It's gotta be only a matter of time, right?

Jana goes upstairs to rest after talking to Atlas in a hushed voice for a few minutes. He nods, they embrace once again, and then she leaves us alone. I don't receive any instructions. Maybe this is part two of a larger test to see if I'm trustworthy.

"So, you've been asleep for three years," Atlas says. He slides a cup of coffee across the pockmarked table. His children peek around the corner into the kitchen. I give them a wave and a smile, and they scatter like mice being caught in the open. "They don't see many strangers."

"Where's their mother?" I say. From the pained expression that creases his lips, the answer is self-evident. I don't push the line of questioning further.

"It's tough surviving out here," Atlas says. "Sometimes you don't."

I avert my eyes and sip the coffee. To my surprise, it's

real. The kitchen is surprisingly well-stocked for being in the middle of the empty plains. A cut of meat cures from a hook over the sink, the faint aroma of cooked onions hangs over the small room. The thin sound of a radio filters in from the den.

"You know you got a hell of a bounty on your head," Atlas says.

I didn't know that, no. "Not surprising," I say with carefree nonchalance. I stir the coffee with the pewter spoon. "What am I worth?"

"Whoever catches you gets full HIVE amenities for life," Atlas says. "The platinum package. Movie star, rock god, President—you get to be whatever you want."

"Sounds like a good deal."

"And you get to bring your friends along too," Atlas says.

"I thought the key would be worth more."

"I don't think they want you back for your Holo-Band," Atlas says. "They've probably reverse engineered HIVE to function without you. Almost, at least."

"Good to know my services are no longer necessary." Then the bounty makes no sense, unless Blackstone is merely trying to make a statement. But he's not the same iron-fisted, *security is everything* demigod that Tanner was. Blackstone doesn't rule through control, but by manipulation and indifference.

"You've been having hallucinations, yes?"

I open my mouth, but find there's not much to say. So we sit in the silence, sipping our coffee, listening to the fridge buzz lightly in the background. Atlas gets up and refills his cup. Rummages around in a few drawers before returning with a small pill.

He places it on the table.

"What's that," I say.

He takes a sip of coffee.

"I studied that drive your brother left behind," Atlas says. "Along with the journal. I understood his plan. It wasn't a bad one. Give each faction a piece of HIVE. Like handing everyone a nuke. Mutually assured destruction keeps everyone in check."

"It didn't work out so well."

"Best solution out of a number of bad ones," Atlas says, stirring a sugar cube into his steaming mug. "You're a gambler. You understand risk."

I consider the destruction left in the wake of my failure and close my eyes. It's tough work, this hero business. Saving the world always has a cost.

"HIVE's worse than even I thought," Atlas says, weariness starting to show in his face. His eyes remain vigilant, but this talk about gambles has the doubts in his mind churning.

"It doesn't really affect you," I say. "I don't think Blackstone's trying to get the Remnants to join."

"You remember the HoloNet?" Atlas says. "Amazing technology. Basically a second brain attached to your own—every piece of information, music, picture you could imagine, at immediate recall."

I recall the sensation of booting it up for the first time and shiver, wrapping my hands around the mug to steady them. A human being wasn't designed to harness all that power. Wasn't meant to know so much at once.

"I used it once or twice," I say. "Not my thing."

Atlas grins at this, like he's found a like-minded soul in a sea of darkness. "Smart man. Now consider if that were a two-way street."

"I don't understand."

Atlas traces his finger along the worn table, outlining as he speaks. "The HoloNet is pretty much one-way. The information downloads into your brain, or you could choose to upload what you wanted to save. Record stuff. But essentially it was a big hard drive repository—lightning fast search and retrieval. Like the old internet, integrated with your mind."

"Right."

"But HIVE built on that. Everyone is still connected—but the information flow is constant, immediate. Imagine a real time, dynamic conversation where a series of monologues once existed. Every thought, every single action, it's all shared in real-time."

I finally suck in my breath and ask the question I want to. "What does this have to do with my hallucinations?"

Atlas gives me a small grin. "I think your brother was smart. Three steps ahead of everyone. No plan is foolproof, but unlike you, he wasn't a gambler. Contingencies upon contingencies. If they ever forced him or you to activate the system, a special program would run."

"And you know this based on what?"

"Analysis of the drive," Atlas says. "I can show you the places in the source code—"

"I'll pass," I say, draining the rest of my coffee. I stand up and refill it on the stove. By the sound of it, it's gonna be a long night. "What's this special program do?"

"I think, eventually, it lets the user know that they're in a simulation. And it burns information—memories—into their subconscious that could be used to find a way to shut the whole thing down." He pauses. "Certain users, at least. Not everyone."

"And why's it even matter," I say. The coffee burns

my tongue when I bring the steaming mug up to my lips. "It just sounds like you're afraid Blackstone is spying on everyone via HIVE. So what."

"That's one scenario," Atlas says. "The ultimate sur-veillance mechanism. But no, the Circle had that down pretty well even before HIVE. Ran a tight ship, as they say. HIVE is overkill for that."

"What then?"

"I think the HIVE infrastructure acts as a conduit to a central mainframe. Imagine a half million or a million brains linked together, all running in parallel. You're not so much jacking into the HIVE as becoming part of it—a worker bee in a massive brain. Or a single neuron, if you prefer."

"A literal hive mind."

"The smartest computer ever created," Atlas says, his finger finally stopping. "A sentient, superhuman AI."

"But it was just a VR program," I say, somewhat con-fused. "Hell of a trick, but it's more…relaxing than dan-gerous."

"I think the simulation is to pacify people," Atlas says. "Save their high-level brainpower for the mainframe. Think about it—all your problems were basically solved, right?"

Life was begrudgingly good in HIVE. I tip back the coffee and cough on the dregs.

"Look, reality is uncomfortable as hell," Atlas says. "Trust me, I know. I'm out here in the frozen winter, miles from civilization, and I'm still shitting my pants about it."

"You're afraid the AI will take over and go rogue?" I say, my throat burning from the grounds.

Atlas shakes his head. "It still comes down to men. Whoever controls that type of power—they'll be able to see a hundred moves ahead. A thousand. Imagine having the counsel of Galileo, Newton, Einstein, multiplied a thousandfold."

My history is a little rusty, but that doesn't sound like a team you'd want to go to war against.

"Why would Matt even build that," I finally say, in barely a whisper.

"Think of the possibilities an AI like that could achieve. It could fix the world in the correct hands. Solve all our problems. Imagine having the intelligence of a thousand Matthew Stokes, all working to benefit humanity."

I nod, but still say, "But it wasn't worth the risk."

"But it was," Atlas says, "because if his first plan failed, your brother had this fail-safe."

"I'll be sure to thank him for that."

Atlas' face darkens. "I don't think your brother can help."

It hasn't really occurred to me, but I'm not shocked when he says it. No reason to keep his consciousness around. "Yeah, I know, Matt's gone."

Which means triggering this fail-safe is really up to me. It's weird, how this ridiculous hallucination I told Jana about is quickly becoming reality.

"I think your brother wanted something more for humanity than just to survive. He wanted us to thrive." Atlas rises suddenly, startling me enough that I almost drop the mug. At first I think it's because something is happening outside—Blackstone's men have tracked us, and we're about to be lit up.

Instead, he gives me a reassuring nod, then disappears

from the room. A creaky door opens and footsteps pad down the basement stairs. I listen to Atlas shuffle around and mutter to himself about where he left everything.

My eyes narrow, focusing on the tiny pill that Atlas retrieved earlier. He still hasn't mentioned what the hell it's for.

Atlas returns, bearing a stack of computer printouts. The veins in his sinewy forearms pop out from the weight out of the papers.

"I managed to compile and analyze the part of the HIVE source your brother left," Atlas says. "Against Vlad's explicit instructions, but you know." He shrugs. "You understand."

He takes the final sheet from the bottom of the stack. Pushing it across the table, he says, "Along the bottom. You see that line of code?"

"I guess," I say, looking at what amounts to nonsense. Computer programming was never my thing. I always considered myself more of a social engineer. "You mind translating?"

"It's the final check before the program runs. It's checking for the HoloBand in your neck—and it looks for either your DNA signature or Matt's."

"I already knew I was the key."

"But underneath it," Atlas says, his finger tracing to the last line of code, "this is a file that was uploaded on to the band. I think it's what's causing your hallucinations. Some of them, at least."

"What do you mean, some of them?"

"Something this complex, there's glitches, you know," Atlas says. "People react in different ways. Some people don't take to it."

I feel he's seeing I have a weak constitution, but I don't pursue the subject. "Jana has the band," I say. "I don't think installing it again is really an option."

"They'd track us here in minutes if we did that," Atlas says. He runs his hand through his gray hair. "But I don't need the HoloBand." He pushes the pill across the table. "All I need is you and your subconscious."

"I'm not taking that." I stare at the crimson tablet. "I don't know what the hell it is."

"Think of it as a way to awaken dormant memories," Atlas says, tapping the side of his temple. "Like the one that Matt's code downloaded into your head the minute you jacked into HIVE."

"Look, man, I'm not taking this," I say. "My head is already fucked up."

I go to rise from my seat. His fingers clamp down on my wrist—kind of like how a dog lets you know that it can hurt you, if need be. But his threat isn't one of physical violence.

"From what I hear, Vlad isn't too fond of you." Atlas raises an eyebrow, confirming this.

I stare at the pill and a ripple of anxiety washes over me. What if it doesn't hold the answers? What if I'm just screwed? I grab it and feel it scratch against my dry throat on the way down.

"How long," I say.

"Not long."

Thirty seconds later, the kitchen disappears.

7 | TENUOUS NOTIONS

REALITY IS A tenuous notion, one constructed of lies and half-truths. Even the world we see, on a very real level, is a lie. The way our optic nerve functions, there's actually a massive chasm in our vision. Our mind creates this image of complete reality by filling in the blanks like a coloring book.

This thought, makes me realize that I'm under the influence of Atlas' pill. Because it's not so much *my* thought as *Matt*'s—a string of his memories and ideas, compressed into a single montage.

Hopefully it's a more detailed version of the fail-safe that Atlas thinks is real. Otherwise not only am I dead, but humanity will suffer, too. And I've had enough flip-book-like hallucinations for one day already.

"You've got the fastest tongue I know. Use it to be clever. Defend yourself by outthinking them." Eight year-old me blinks across the table, grubby from getting beaten up and embarrassed day after day. That moment must have been important to Matt, too. Then the scene shifts, whirling through Matt's life. Early days at Gifted Minds, some fun experiments with Andrew Marshwood.

The sensation is somewhere between watching a film

and experiencing it. The memory reel speeds up, so fast that I can't make out distinct moments. I see Chancellor Tanner, the Origin Point, Inner Circle meetings. These apparently hold little value in this little memory story. I suspect they are only there for contrast—to remind me of what is at stake should I not fix HIVE.

Nothing stops until close to the end—a week before Matt ultimately died. He's distributing the HIVE source drives, intent on creating a stalemate that will bring some semblance of equality between the factions—or, if some good-hearted person is clever enough, a better tomorrow on the back of the HIVE mind.

Midway through, after his visit to the Remnants, Matt takes a detour. One not mentioned in his journal, or un-covered by any of those trying to track his movements.

Matthew Stokes travels to the Western Stronghold. A hundred miles south of Seattle, close enough to our old home that it hurts.

He—I—wipes the dust off a sign, the weather-worn letters scraping against my palm. It reads GIFTED MINDS RESEARCH INSTITUTE, WESTERN DIVI-SION. Just like my hallucination, but this time less dis-concerting. More tangible.

It's proof.

Finally, the memory flashes to a single sheet of paper. I see the hand trace out triple helixes—Matt's insignia—and then a stream of words flow across the crinkled sur-face from the fountain pen.

If the wrong person gets HIVE, a good man will know what to do.

Then everything goes black.

*

I WAKE UP covered in sweat, mumbling to myself. Atlas pats me on the shoulder, and I recoil.

"It confirmed what you thought," Atlas says. It's not a question. I assume, somewhere in his streams of data analysis, that he already drew this conclusion long ago. He was simply waiting for me to arrive in order to prove that the fail-safe existed.

Some gamble. A million things could've gone differently, with me never reaching him. What then? Would he have tried to piece together an image from the code, translate the ones and zeroes into a memory?

No. He didn't need me to prove its existence.

He needs me to go and find it. Because soon, he will die—and his kids don't have a mother to look after them while their old man spends his last days sifting through ash.

I breathe heavily, trying to regain my composure. He hands me a cup of iced coffee. I drain it in one gulp and sit upright. The farmhouse's kitchen comes back into focus. A simple wooden table, the buzz of the decades-old refrigerator.

Through the open door to the hallway, I can see two pairs of eyes peeking out, filled not with fear, but with wonder.

"Your dad has amazing drugs," I call out.

Atlas slaps me on the ear. "Jana said you were a wise ass."

"It's kept me alive."

"Can't argue with that." He helps me to my feet. It takes a minute to get my bearings, but soon the room is just a room. Familiar old reality.

Well, not quite. There's a dog in the corner panting who looks suspiciously like Ramses. He barks when I look at him.

"You don't have a dog, do you?"

"No," Atlas says. "We had to put him down last year." He turns toward the corner, following my gaze. "The hallucinations are getting worse, aren't they?"

I stare the smiling dog in the face and say, "Fuck."

Atlas disappears, leaving me with Ramses. The dog sidles over, and I feel every bit of his hundred-pound frame against my leg.

I find myself whispering, "This isn't real, this isn't real."

Atlas returns, and Ramses even turns to look at the newcomer. Growls at him. I rub my forehead and try to stare at the ceiling. But the endless panting echoes in my ears no matter how much I try to ignore it.

He has a thick red folder filled with printouts. Atlas sifts through them, muttering.

"Yes, I think there's a glitch in the code," Atlas says, after what seems like hours. He hands me one of the sheets. "Line 267,762. You see it?"

"Just explain it to me."

He rubs his gray hair and shrugs. "I understand. It's been a long day for you."

Ramses barks, and I jump. "I'm not a computer programmer, so if you could—"

"It's hard to tell whether your brother meant to do this, or if it was simply a slip," Atlas says. "Almost every line of the program is flawless."

"So it's a feature, not a bug."

Atlas raises his eyebrow at me. "Thought you said you didn't code."

"I lived with someone who did for a long time," I say, remembering Matt's nerdy T-shirts. "I heard all about it."

"I think it's to remind certain people," Atlas says. "That the real world is better than HIVE."

So maybe it's not that my constitution is weak after all.

In the ultimate ironic twist, I just love authenticity so much that my brain is violently rejecting the pleasantness of a fake existence.

"So it'll go away?"

"Who knows," Atlas says. "In the beginning, when they rolled out HIVE, there were a few…complications."

"You mean deaths."

"Yes," Atlas says. "It seems some people's minds just aren't built for such stimuli. Consider hallucinogens. One man becomes a monk, gaining infinite insight. Another man thinks he's a glass of orange juice for the rest of his miserable days."

"Lovely," I say, watching Ramses chase his tail. "And the cure?"

"Wait it out," Atlas says. "I wish I had something else to offer." He reaches over the stack of papers and extracts a single sheet. Hands it to me. "Keep this safe. And get to the Gray Desert as quickly as you can." He points upstairs. "Get some rest. You'll need it."

I don't protest. I fold the paper into a rectangle and then slide it into my back pocket. As I trudge wearily up the stairs, eyes beginning to grow heavy, I do wonder about Atlas' tone when he said *you'll need it.*

What's coming next that requires me to be well-rested?

8 | AFTERMATH

MY QUESTION IS answered the next morning when I wake up handcuffed in a swamp of my own sweat.

"You can't be serious," I say, twisting to evade Jana's grasp. But she wordlessly drags me out of bed and down to the truck. We're on the road before the sun even comes up. It feels a little unfair, being had in my sleep.

"You're not going to say anything?" I shake my hands after five minutes of silence pass. "So that's how it's gonna be? Come on, we don't have to kill the old man. You can just let me go."

I'm also a little annoyed at Atlas for not giving me more warning. I thought we'd bonded. Not that I could've stopped her. All that military engineering would crush me. But not even giving me a chance feels a little unsporting.

Plus, when it's necessary, I can run pretty damn fast.

So now I'm chained to the truck's glove box at a rather uncomfortable angle. One that doesn't even allow me the luxury of leaning back into the seat.

"We talked about this," I say, rattling the cuffs. They clink against the plastic. Jana shoots me a look that tells me if I try anything, she's going to put my head through the window. "I thought you trusted me."

"I believe you," she says. "Trust is another matter entirely."

"You talked with Atlas, right? You know I'm not leading you on."

"So he says." There's a long pause. "He also mentioned you're seeing things."

"Fuck you," I say, and put my both of feet against the plastic dashboard, using them as leverage to pull backwards. The front heaves and cracks, threatening to come off. I feel the truck swerve off road slightly as Jana reaches over to stop me.

I struggle against her hand, but she's too strong. Goddamn science experiments. "This how you treat all your partners?"

"The ones I can't trust, yeah."

"We had a deal."

"I don't know about that," she says. "But you're the one who says we needed to gather an army. And this is the way to do it."

I don't see how putting me in handcuffs makes that task any easier. The only good thing about this situation is that no imaginary dogs or memory snippets are encroaching on my tenuous grip on reality.

"Don't tell me you're—"

"I'm taking you to Vlad. For your trial."

"If you want to kill me, then do it now," I say.

"Our people have a process," she says, not bothering to explain further. "If I disappear, they'll follow. I must face them. Him."

"Cool," I say. "We'll face him together. Uncuffed." My feet slide off the dash. Her grip relaxes, and an uneasy calm settles over the cab.

"I've already delayed your trial enough," Jana says. "I can't put it off any more."

"Try harder."

"There wasn't going to be one at all. I got word last night that Vlad had accepted my compromise. Even getting him to entertain the idea of—what, an implanted memory—was almost impossible. He just wanted to execute you. Seeing as how you're not worth much any more."

"Check the news," I say. "There's a big bounty on me."

"Not one that can help us, Luke," she says. "It is what it is."

"How refreshing," I say. "Remind me why I'm trying to help you miserable assholes at all."

"Because it's the only way you can save yourself."

I run my tongue over my teeth and shut my mouth. The truck bumps and grinds over the pitted road, each pothole making the cuffs cut into my wrists. Most people spend their entire lives searching for someone who sees straight through them. What they don't realize, though, is it's not quite what you expect it to be.

"Relax, Luke."

"Easy for you to say. You're not about to die."

"I'll make Vlad understand."

"And if you can't?"

"Then you better think of a contingency," she says, catching my eye in the rearview. "But you're already working on that, right?"

I don't answer, just try to tune out the groan of the engine by looking out the window and thinking happy thoughts. Only problem is, in a life filled with very few, the darkness seeps in pretty quick.

"Can I trust you to make him understand?" I say. "Tell me you'll do what we discussed earlier."

There's a long, still silence, punctuated only by the rusty gears and punch of the truck's old diesel engine. I desperately want to close my eyes, but the fragmentary hallucinations have me paranoid. Reality is a frightening enough proposition for the human animal without seeing things that aren't there.

"However bad you thought your life was," Jana says, with a quiet grit, "It's nothing like ours."

Fucking solidarity.

She's going to stick with her people.

When you live day-by-day, life is but a series of temporary ordeals. Nasty, brutish and short. A permanent cure to extend the pain is neither desirable or even within the capacity of understanding.

I curl up against the window and close my eyes. No visions come.

I think about trust, and how relying on others always bites me in the ass.

And I decide that Jana Rose is right.

I'll just have to make Vlad understand myself.

One way or another.

9 | TRIAL

I'M WOKEN BY a pistol's snout jabbing me in the ribs. I stumble from the truck's cab without protest, awkwardly wiping sleep from my eyes as I take in the surroundings. Midday light seeps through the gray sky, casting an ominous pall over the bleak horizon.

"So this is the Gunpowder Hills," I say. Jana's already gone. Hopefully to grovel to Vlad, and convince him that I'm their one and only hope. But seeing this place, I don't feel that hope is even in the Remnants' vocabulary. Somewhere like this, it would be a suicidal ideal to uphold.

"Move it, traitor," Mirko says with gruff insistence, almost sending me into the dirt. Now acclimated to his rough tricks, I manage to stand upright. "You're about to get what's fit for a dog like you."

I'm herded past a crowd of Remnants leaning up against a section of the outer gate which has been fashioned from two-story crushed cars. They shoot me a look of utter disgust. But there are bigger problems—like what's inside the gates. Steel creaks and groans, forming an open channel just wide enough to fit a cargo truck. A dirt bike heads my way through the narrow corridor of twisted metal.

I shield my eyes from the high beams. My heart pounds, but I don't try to dive out of the bike's path. Been through too much to run and hide. Two feet before the bike kneecaps me, the driver brings it to a screeching kick stop. A shower of rocks bounces off my face.

I blink, but don't move. The grip on my shoulder tightens as Mirko stands at attention. I know I'm expected to demonstrate the same reverence. But I make it a point not to, even though deep down I'm wondering what the hell it's like to die. Wondering just why the hell Jana decided to go with option one after all.

Then again, dying shouldn't be that scary. If death is simply the experience of unreality, then I've been well-prepared by the past three years. But philosophical notions die hard when you're smacked in the face with the stench of gas, sweat and fear.

The rider dismounts. He wears all black, his green eyes shining out from beneath the endless folds of fabric. His outfit is punctuated by a thin red band around his neck that resembles a rugged scarf. The bike purrs behind him. Guess he's prepared to make a quick getaway if I don't have what he wants.

"So we finally meet," the man says, his gaze fixated on me as he steps closer. We're almost nose-to-nose. He's a little taller than me, heavier, too. Or it could be the clothing. "You've caused me a lot of trouble."

"Don't tell me I'm the reason this shithole exists." I gesture toward the compound, past the massive walls of scrap.

"My daughter warned me about your smart mouth." A gleaming pistol materializes from beneath his flowing garb. But the gun's pointed the wrong way, the barrel gripped between his fingers. The stock rushes out, catching me in the temple and sending me face-first to the ground.

Daughter.

"You're Vlad," I say, my mouth feeling like it's full of cotton balls. I reach out to grab his pant leg, but he brushes me away. Blood dribbles from my mouth into the ruined soil. I get to my knees, feeling the coarse dirt mixing with the open wound.

"Consider this your trial," Vlad says with a detached cool. When I look up, I see black fabric flapping in the gentle wind. I'm suddenly aware that many of the Gunpowder Hills' citizens have filtered out of the gates.

"Your brother was our savior," Vlad says, with a shocking amount of reverence. "But we'd be foolish to believe you're cut from the same cloth."

"You're not the first one I've fooled," I say, unable to resist. Bracing myself for the inevitable lash of his pistol, I'm surprised when, instead, Vlad drags me up and dusts me off. His eyes search mine, and I detect the faintest hint of amusement—like this situation has a certain air of tragic comedy that only the two of us have noticed.

"We're a fair sort," Vlad says. "You got a minute to explain why we shouldn't execute you."

About to topple over, woozy from the first smack to the head, I search the crowd for answers. Hundreds of green eyes stare back at me, some from bare heads, others from behind the thick fabric protecting them from the harsh plains.

No solutions reveal themselves. I look for Evelyn and Carina—or even Jana—but find no respite in the throng of unfamiliar faces. Strangely, my heart doesn't hammer or skip.

I offer an easy shrug. "I don't think there's a compelling case."

My honesty throws him off. He opens his mouth to respond, then closes it. Finally, he says, "Twenty seconds, Mr. Stokes. Your life could be a short one."

I stroke my chin. The cuffs rattle lightly. What life awaits me, even if I manage to survive? Constant struggle doesn't sound particularly wonderful. But then, that's what life has always been, always will be: a series of insurmountable challenges that just about break us.

Unless you don't let 'em.

"Five seconds."

"Because I have the cure to your disease," I say. I feel the crowd tense. Years of scraping by has taught them to be cautious. "Not what Ford did to you. What everyone else is *gonna* do."

A murmur bursts through the crowd at the mention of Damien Ford's unspoken atrocities. Suffice to say, he's not revered in these parts. It takes a little contorting, but I remove the paper Atlas gave me from my back pocket. It flutters in the slight breeze when I reach out to hand it to Vlad.

"Zero," Vlad says with expressionless nonchalance. "Time's up."

"Read it."

"Perhaps you should have stated your case more eloquently."

"You want to stop running, you better read the fucking paper," I say, turning around slowly so that everyone gets a look at my face. I brandish the paper above my head, like it holds the secrets to life itself. In truth, I haven't looked at what Atlas gave me. It could be nothing. Or it could be proof that I'm worth more than an entertaining public spectacle. "Anyone know what that is? *Living*? What you know is *survival*. This is your ticket out."

And mine too—but that's irrelevant. When you make the sale, it's always about what they want. And this, well, it's what I would call a compelling offer. Door number one—executing me to sate their bloodlust, that outcome is known. The Remnants will continue being hunted by the recently formed New Allied States. But door number two promises change. Maybe disaster, perhaps indescribable joy—either way, life will never be the same.

I set my feet into the cracked soil and stare at Vlad. "So."

Vlad finally takes the paper and opens it. "Who gave you this?"

"You said it yourself," I say, "My brother was your savior. This is straight from him. He wrote the code. I'm just delivering the message."

It's difficult arguing with your own words. Particularly when you've made a proclamation to your entire tribe. Vlad carefully creases the paper down the middle and places it inside a fold in his desert garments.

"This will be taken to the council." Vlad smiles and gets on the bike. "We'll have a decision by tonight."

He revs the engine and speeds away, leaving me coughing. The crowd disperses, everyone throwing hasty glances toward me. I feel Mirko's rough hands around my neck. Then I'm dragged away, through the narrow metal gates, into the heart of the Gunpowder Hills.

10 | FIEFDOM

I ONLY CATCH a brief glimpse of the Remnants' fiefdom as I'm pulled through the dusty streets. Gas-powered lamps flicker in the hazy afternoon light. Generators hum and crackle. A thin smog hangs over the settlement, from all the families in tight proximity.

The scent of life permeates everything. It's not ugly, but it's also not pleasant. This is what strikes me as most unreal—and yet, most appealing—about my time in HIVE. Everything smelled beautiful. But alas, life is messier. Far more similar to the third or fourth fuck of the night than the glorious first.

Mirko and his fellow soldiers pull me to the end of one of the narrow streets and toss me inside a single-story residence that resembles the others.

Mirko walks inside and takes a small key from his pocket.

It dangles in front of my nose as he says, "Hold your hands up."

I offer him my cuffed wrists. "So you decided to let me go," I say. "Well done."

"Don't get your hopes up."

The building shakes as Mirko bolts the door from the outside.

There's a knock at the door.

"Miss me already?" I say. When I squint to look at my dark surroundings, the cut at my temple hurts.

"You best pray," his gruff voice says with relish. "If that's your thing."

Mirko's buddy says, "The council don't overturn nothing."

"You were a dead man the minute you came here, Stokes," Mirko says. There's a long pause. "And don't drink the water."

With that, they stomp away, leaving me in a square, almost empty room. Haggard beams of light scrape and claw their way in through a shoebox-sized window in the far corner. It's just as well that the place isn't brimming with illumination. A rat scurries over my foot as I walk toward the rickety bench along the wall.

I don't even jump. I'm too tired to be bothered.

"They caught you too, eh buddy?" I say to my four-legged friend.

The rat hisses, its green eyes probing the depths of my tortured soul before it plunges into a hole. Damien Ford, it would seem, did a number on everything in these parts. Or so the books said—the official record can be unreliable at best. It's hard to believe one man is responsible for laying waste to an entire section of a country.

Aside from the bench, there's a tiny furnace in the corner and a stack of wood. Some water sits in a pot on the single burner stove. Tasting dried blood, I head to the stove in order to wash up. Touching the water with my cracked fingertips makes me realize how frigid and tired I truly am. Adrenaline dulls the true nature of your surroundings, but it always subsides. Now, I am staring reality in the face for the first time in three years.

The realization is powerful enough that I almost have to sit down. Instead, with shaking hands, I place logs inside the furnace. Take a little kindling from the nearby pile, arrange it just so. Work the striker until the pile erupts into a crackling ball of flame.

I stare into the rusted pot. The water looks normal.

I'm tempted to drink it straight away, but Mirko's strange warning gives me pause. So I step away and, as I walk toward the bench, I crumple to one knee. Hallucinations jump across my vision.

The pot hisses and spits, boiling over. How much time has passed? *Sizzle*. Steam fills the air.

The bursts of light continue as I clutch my knees to my chest. Ramses, Evelyn, Carina, Seattle— they all pass by in a blur. Matt's memories—of the Gifted Minds Institute, of his efforts to distribute HIVE—pulse in between the hallucinations. Mostly colors, fragments of a ruined scrapbook. I see a final image, this one clear. An old highway sign. I5.

When I open my eyes, I'm covered in sweat on the dirty floor. The small space is filled with the acrid scent of torched metal. I stagger over to the stove and take the empty pot off. It burns my hand, and I scream.

The door opens.

"I thought you were dying," Jana says in a hushed whisper as the ancient hinge creaks. "The guard called me over. You look like hell."

"See how you look after you've been in jail."

"I don't think that's it." She comes closer. The glow of the dying fire gives the tattoo on her face a little color.

"You come to apologize?"

"Why?" She reaches into her waistband and takes out a bottle of water. Tosses it to me. Even though the throw is slow as hell, I drop it. "What do I have to be sorry for?"

I don't answer, since I'm busy scrambling for the water. Once I get the cap off, I drink the entire thing in a single gulp. Liquid streams down my chin. I can taste blood and dirt, but it doesn't matter. This drink is about the best one I've had in my life.

When my thirst is sated, I realize how much my palm hurts from the pot. One problem solved, another one immediately steps in to assume the mantle.

"No rest for the wicked," I say beneath my breath.

"What's that?"

"Nothing," I say. "Life's funny."

"Yeah, it's hilarious," Jana says. She scowls when she finds the blackened pot. "You try to burn the place down?"

"Why are you here?"

"I came to explain my plan."

"Oh," I say, starting a slow clap, only to immediately regret it. "Since you're so good at following plans."

"You can't just walk up and kill Vlad. There are *rules*."

"Clearly," I say.

"That's not how things work around here," she says. "You don't understand."

"Try me."

"Forget it," she says, and turns to leave.

I rush over, not because I'm so eager to talk, but because I'm thinking about something else. I grab her arm lightly and say, "Sorry."

"Don't try this bullshit on me, Luke."

"What's that?"

"I saw your little harem. They're staying across the street."

"You give me a little too much credit," I say, dropping my hand from her wrist. "I want to hear the plan."

"You do?"

"I mean shit, sending you best chance of survival within an inch of the gallows is brilliant. I've gotta know more."

"Fuck you," Jana says.

"You should trust me." I put my hand on her shoulder, making sure her eyes are locked with mine. With my other hand, I work through the folds in her clothing. I'm not sure what I'm hunting for, but any tools I don't have are a good place to start. "I saved your life, remember?"

"But you're not family."

"Your family is gonna get you killed." My fingers snake past a leather scabbard. *Knife.* That could be helpful. But I'm greedy, and keep moving. Because I remember she has something that will force her to go all-in, plans be damned.

The HoloBand.

See, we're still at the point where there's still an idea in her head that, maybe, her father was right all along. The plan may have changed—since I'm no longer a tradable asset for anything worthwhile to the Remnants—but the sentiment remains. If the first plan was a good one, then his new plan, to execute me as a message to everyone else, must also be sound.

So I think a little demonstration is in order. Symbolism is clearly big amongst the Remnants, and this will make a clear statement. About what I truly think about the direction their faction is headed.

She moves slightly, and I almost bump into her waist. Instead, I pinch her shoulder.

"Ow, what the hell."

"I'm trying to bring you back to reality, here," I say. Got it. The HoloBand, in its little protective case, is in her back pocket. Nothing to it. Easy trick. My fingers pass by the scabbard again, and I can't resist. I push slightly on her skin with my visible hand, my fingers tracing her shoulder. "Right here."

"Don't do this, Luke," she says, her breath getting softer. "I can't. I have a plan."

"You still haven't said much about that." I reach my head closer, toward her lips. At the last moment, she pushes me away. I quickly palm the HoloBand as I stumble backwards. A loud expletive masks the clatter of the knife.

I fall on the blade to cover it up, pretending to be hurt.

"You could've just said you weren't interested." I hold up my arm, where the knife nicked me. Blood runs down. It looks a lot worse than it is. But, then again, that was the plan. I knew she wouldn't kiss me. Her heart is beating a million different ways, and she doesn't even like me. That's a luxury the plains don't afford.

"I need to go," she says, her face flushed. She pauses before she reaches the door. "I was going to get Atlas to testify on your behalf. That was the plan."

"Then you should've brought him along for the ride."

"I didn't think of it until now," she says, and then rushes out of the room.

Which is when I realize that I've been wrong about one thing.

The Remnants do hope, they do dream, they do imagine, they do plan—just like anyone else.

They're just not very good at it.

I wipe the blood off my arm and test the tip of the knife. I'm not sure where the blade will land, but I am sure of one thing.

I'm not accepting any verdicts without a damn fight.

11 | REGICIDE

FIGHTING MAY BE difficult. I'm still dehydrated, mentally disoriented, and generally feel like I'm battling the worst flu of my life. It's hard to formulate any sort of plan. Who do I even want to kill? Where do I hide my ill-gotten new tools?

A knock at the door startles me. I hurry to hide the knife. The best place I can settle on is my waistband. The cool metal presses against my bare skin. Any sudden movement, and I'm going to open up a nice cut around my groin. Not the best positioning, but it's the best I can do on short notice. I slip the HoloBand into my pocket just as Mirko enters.

"Man, you look like shit."

I look down at the dried blood caking my arm and say, my throat ragged, "I don't know what happened."

He shrugs. "They said you were gonna be crazy after being hooked up to that machine. Scratching and clawing at yourself like a dog."

"You come to watch the freak show?"

He grimaces. "It's been three hours. The council made its decision."

Mirko grabs me by the shoulder. He doesn't bother

to recuff me, since I'm too weak to offer even token resistance. It takes all my energy to simply walk as we travel through the winding streets. Green eyes peek through the metallic shutters and junk.

"Move," Mirko says.

"I'm trying," I say.

"Don't try," he says. "Move."

It's like I forgot how to walk. My mind is scattered in a million directions, my senses unreliable. Great job, Matt, inventing something that destroys basic motor movements. A stunning achievement. Some minutes later, Mirko flings me forward. It's dark in here. Or maybe my eyes are shut. I heave in and out, trying to catch my breath.

I remember what Atlas told me. I need to get to the Gray Desert. Otherwise these hallucinations are going to ruin what's left of my brain.

"Here." It's Vlad. He waves something in front of my nostrils, and I recoil. It's like being jacked into an electrical socket.

I stand bolt upright, hands tingling as I scan the large meeting room. Thick wooden benches are lined up before where Vlad sits on a stage a couple feet off the ground. He sits on a large chair on a crescent-shaped three-foot-tall riser. Chairs fan out around his pedestal, each occupied by a person dressed in similar black robes. He's the only one with a crimson scarf, though.

"This a church?"

"Depends on your definition of church," Vlad says. I'm beginning to think the Remnants' garments were adopted as a uniform, rather than for practical reasons.

"The council, I presume."

"A verdict has been reached on the actions of one Lucas Stokes," Vlad says.

"That's not my name," I say.

Vlad waves me off. "We have reviewed the paper, and taken it into consideration."

"Before you tell me the verdict, you should know something," I say. In the back of my mind, I'm thinking that I don't want to die here. Anywhere but here.

"It won't change anything."

I don't like the sound of that, but I say anyway, "I know exactly where to look." The last image, painful as it was to channel—or whatever the hell you want to call it—gave me a precise idea of where Matt hid the fail-safe. The I5 sign confirmed it. I know the area.

I can take them there, if they'll let me.

"It's irrelevant," Vlad says. "No further evidence will be reviewed."

"You're signing your own damn death warrant." The other council members stiffen. Such outspoken criticism isn't tolerated. They survive by tribal law, the ones that man grew up with, before the plains were lost, before he harnessed fire and bent the world to his whim.

Vlad steps down from his perch. His measured steps echo. I lean against one of the benches for support, looking for an opening. Nothing comes, and so when he's only a few yards away, I pull the trigger on a half-cocked plan.

"Back the fuck up," I scream, reaching for my pocket. "You need me."

I hold up the stolen HoloBand capsule. The plastic catches the soft light.

Vlad stops, amusement flickering in his bright eyes.

"We don't need that." There's a murmur of assent from the group. "We don't need you."

"But you're big on ritual. And respect." With a single squeeze, I crush the HoloBand in my sweaty palm. A jolt surges through me—the realization that this is the last remaining tangible piece of Matt. But there's no time for sentimentality.

My symbolic act of defiance has made the council upset. One member stands rigid. Her robes fall away, and I see the familiar rose tattoo.

"You will not interrupt," Jana says.

Vlad turns, perhaps to reprimand his daughter for speaking out of turn during the ceremony. It's clear now that he only rose from the stage to execute me. Pulling the knife out from my waistband so quickly that I cut my skin, I rush forward. Vlad looks back just in time for me to catch him in the chest. The blade slices through the fabric effortlessly.

A sputtered protest spills from his lips. "You…you will destroy everything."

Blood drips down the hilt of the knife. Then Vlad's green eyes go blank, like a lamp suddenly being unplugged. For a moment, the council members don't move, everyone disbelieving the new reality unfolding before them.

The blood feels warm and slick on my hands. I let go of the knife, and Vlad topples over. The hilt clangs off the stone, setting off a flurry of activity. The council members rise, ready to converge and tear me limb from limb.

I focus on Jana, who stares blankly past me. This was not the plan either of us had in mind, but it was the best one available under the circumstances. I back up, wondering if I can make it to the door before the council rip me apart. They stalk forward, forming a tight line between the rows of benches.

"You son of a bitch," Jana says, with a venom I'm not quite expecting. "I had a plan."

"And I told you we had to kill him."

"This wasn't the plan," she repeats, like it means something.

"Next time actually have a plan," I say, scanning my adversaries, their glowing eyes focused on me with a singular purpose.. "One that didn't involve convincing a group of morons."

A rumbling growl erupts from one of the black-robed throats. I can't tell who it is, because, frankly, they all resemble feral dogs in their one-mindedness. My boot catches on a loose stone, and I stumble backwards.

It's ignominious to scramble and grovel, so I slide along the floor, keeping a cool distance between me and the council. More of a symbolic gesture, since only a few yards separate us. They're drawing it out on purpose. The member at the head of the line unsheathes his sword.

"Stop," Jana says. The group tilts their heads, unsure if they should listen. "As your leader, I command you to stop." To my surprise, they obey, giving me time to stand. Jana finally begins to move, pushing through the throng until she's eye-to-eye with me, just the two of us standing before the onlookers.

"You gave me no choice," I say. "Contingencies, right?"

"To hell with your contingencies," Jana says. I'm not sure whether she's here to kill me herself, or about to break down crying in my arms. Her body quakes with unbridled emotion.

"He killed your mother."

"Don't talk about my mother," Jana says, her gaze white-hot. "Don't ever talk about her."

"All right, all right," I say, raising my hands in a peace offering. "Look, I'm sorry—"

"No you're not."

"You're right." I say. "It was him or me."

"You made your choice. Now I'll make mine."

I don't have a response for that. Rustiness. Reading the situation wrong. I thought she was pissed because she just became an orphan. Rather, she's pissed because this is the messiest transition of power that could possibly go down.

After a long silence, she nods to the rest of the council. "Tell everyone we ship out tomorrow."

The council doesn't move or answer.

Jana brings her foot down against the stone with a thunderous boom. "Tell them they can either come or go. But we leave for the Gray Desert at daybreak."

There's a hushed, involuntary gasp as the council members hurry past us. I tense up, still wary. After all, two minutes before they were ready to feast on my limbs. Or whatever the customs are around here. But soon the meeting room is empty, leaving me and Jana alone.

"I'll help bury him," I say. Because, really, what do you say in this situation?

"No," she says. "I'll bury the bastard alone."

It's not open for debate. So I leave the new queen of the Remnants by herself, and exit into the chilly air.

Tomorrow, we head to the Gray Desert.

Tomorrow, the flashbacks might end.

Or tomorrow might bring a whole new host of problems that today I knew nothing about.

12 | FIELDS OF OPPORTUNITY

I DRIVE THE truck. Jana, always talkative, says nothing in the passenger seat. I check the mirrors, watching the procession trailing behind us on the cracked highway. It can't be more than a thousand people.

After the call went out over the Remnants' network, this is who agreed to come. Ten percent. The rest stayed with Mirko. I think that says a lot about what will befall them.

But then, throwing in with Jana doesn't look much better. Two days after getting my life back, it's already over. An army of a thousand against Blackstone's and the NAS' millions won't get it done.

I play with the satellite radio, but all I get is empty white noise. The ash hanging in the atmosphere must block the reception. We've traveled for about five hours, and the sky has gotten progressively chalkier. Even three years later, the plains haven't recovered.

And we've only reached the border of what used to be Illinois. Or so a battered sign indicates, announcing that the people of Iowa welcome us with fields of opportunities. But the only fields I see are gray.

It makes me snort, thinking that there are opportunities here. But that's what I'm searching for, right? A silver bullet in an endless cosmic ocean of ash.

I asked Evelyn to examine me before we left—maybe help with these hallucinations—but she brushed me off. No one likes me much these days. They just tolerate me as a necessary sort of evil.

Being a hero is a thankless business.

I jerk the wheel to avoid a ten-foot-deep hole, blaring on the horn to warn those behind us. Jana has insisted that we lead the procession, even if that leaves us open to attack. No one's attacked us thus far, which might be disappointing her. After all, she's gotta channel this anger somewhere.

Preferably not at me.

"Was it real?" she says after another hundred miles.

"Was what real?" I say, startled that she's speaking. If I'm being perfectly honest, the silence was preferable.

"Or were you just trying to—that was my knife," she says, putting the dots together without my help. She smiles bitterly and runs her hand through her punkish hair. "I'm a fucking moron."

"Next time, don't change the plan."

The silence makes me wonder if I've made another enemy. I can't really afford that, but it seems inevitable. I try to focus on sunnier things, like the fail-safe Matt hid out in the Gifted Minds facility. But it's hard to even imagine. Trying to get inside the mind of a genius is a fool's errand. Even those close to him, close to HIVE, couldn't account for all his plans.

I swallow hard when I realize that Blackstone has a solid brain trust on his side—the remnants of the Gifted Minds program. Kid Vegas. Olivia Redmond. Who knows who else. Either I need to get smarter, or I need a better team.

I bite my lip and push down on the accelerator.

"Do I need to drive?"

"No," I say.

"Then conserve gas," Jana says. "We might have to push anyway."

"There something you want to say?"

"I don't know," Jana says. "What *can* I say?"

"You got what you wanted."

"I wanted my people to be safe."

"Some of them are," I say. I catch her pained response in the rearview as she contemplates the Remnants who stayed behind in the Gunpowder Hills with Mirko. Fortifying, trying to dig in. Even members of the way stations rode in. The rift might've hurt Jana worse than her father's death.

All I see is a bunch of fools about to commit suicide, steamrolled by the inevitable march of the NAS' collective forces.

"We're making the right play," I say. Up ahead, I see a big dog in the road. He's barking. "Shit." I close my eyes and drive straight through. There's no *thud*, because the dog isn't real. "How far until we hit I5?"

"1,800 miles," Jana says. "Should be fun."

I take a deep breath and gather myself. But deep inside, I'm screaming.

Because I don't know if I'm not gonna last that long.

*

WE FINALLY STOP for the night near the border of South Dakota. The vehicle brigade—about three hundred strong—forms a tight perimeter around a central camp. The Remnants waste little time setting up defenses, digging holes and making fires.

I leave them alone. This is their area of expertise, and I'm liable to slow things down. I managed to drive the entire day—the better part of twelve hours—without devolving into madness. But who knows how long this interlude of sanity will last.

From the way Atlas was talking, things will only get worse.

I take the piece of paper he gave me from my back pocket. It's stained by Vlad's blood, but it's a damn good thing I thought to retrieve it before Jana interred him. It might only be a single sheet, but there's a lot of good information on here. Some of it I can't read, since it's computer code, but what's in plain English is still damn important.

"What do you have?" Evelyn says, her voice startling me. I'm off by a spindly tree. It's the kind of place you don't expect visitors. "Just like our old spot in Seattle, right?"

"Ev…"

"I know it wasn't real," she says. "I'm a big girl."

"That's not what I meant." Even in the dark, with the fires a ways off, she cuts a striking image. Long blond hair cascading down to her well-proportioned hips. Endless brown eyes that you could drown in, if you're not careful.

"What's on the paper?"

"Something I got from a friend."

"Now I know you're lying," she says. I smell the faintest hint of lilac carried on the breeze, and it brings me back to all those times in HIVE. And the time outside, in the real world. Her apartment. "You don't have any friends."

"So you two hate me too?"

"The church mouse? I don't think she could hate anyone." This must be what she calls Carina, which I find slightly amusing. Evelyn steps forward, and now the aroma of lilac is overwhelming. I wonder how she manages to smell good, even out here, where beauty has vanished. "She told me something interesting, though."

"What's that?"

"That she loved you."

I don't have an answer ready for this type of situation, so I say, "The paper, it's about—these images. And some other stuff."

"Flashbacks, kind of." Evelyn nods, giving me a little knowing grin. But she lets me off the hook about Carina, which I'm thankful for. A small act of mercy, but it seems like a big one, given how things have gone over the past days. "I've had a few."

"Anything bad?"

"You remember Ramses?"

"Yeah," I say. "I've been seeing him more than I'd like."

"It hasn't been bad for me, Luke," Evelyn says. "But Carina, she's not taking it too well."

"Maybe she's lovesick," I say, immediately regretting the joke. A light wind whistles past, rustling the tree's dead branches.

"Don't be an ass."

"Sometimes that's hard."

"I believe that," Evelyn says. "The flashbacks. Cold sweats. I've been taking care of her."

"Sounds familiar," I say. "Besides anyone taking care of me."

"You can take care of yourself," she says, and reaches over to touch my arm. "Figure out what's on the paper."

"You don't want to know more?"

"I don't know if I could trust what you tell me anyway." Her fingers slide away from my skin. "But I think you're decent enough to do something close to right."

She walks away. I watch as the breeze rustles her flowing blonde hair and smile. Not quite a ringing endorsement, but out here, it'll have to do.

I turn my attention back to the paper. It gives me an engineer's view on how to solve the current problems. Why Atlas believes the conflict started in the first place—belief. What everyone is seeking: salvation.

And how to break free of the cycle.

By giving everyone exactly what they want. It's as cryptic as it sounds. No explanation about what people want, or how to find out. At the bottom is a warning about HIVE: *you can't just pull the plug. The light of civilization will go out.*

I feel a strange power course through my veins when I read the words and stare at the code. I'm the last chance the world has. Not by fate, or talent, but perhaps just by circumstance.

Not really a hero.

Just someone doing what's close to right.

And that, I think, is in the rarest supply of all in this new world.

13 | SURVIVORS

TWO DAYS LATER, we roll through what used to be South Dakota without any problems. Unlike my last trip through the Lost Plains, this one has been uneventful—although calling it pleasant would be inaccurate. The temperatures at night are sub-zero, and black-ice slows our journey. But our convoy moves on without much trouble. A couple vehicles break down beyond repair, reminding everyone that traveling without backup isn't where you want to be.

I've been out of HIVE for all of a week, and I can't say that I've enjoyed coming back to reality.

I pull into an abandoned way station—the last one in the Lost Plains, about three-hundred miles from the border of the Gray Desert—and cut the truck's engine. With the heater off, a bone-chilling frost settles into the cab within minutes. I check my rifle as Jana slowly wakes up.

"Why's it so damn cold?"

"We're at the last way station," I say.

"Anyone here?" But the words are said without much hope, and don't require any answer. The convoy stops behind us, spread out in a haphazard fashion. The tight circles and night watches that marked our early journey have yielded to a weary complacency.

I adjust the knife hanging from my belt. Jana gave it to me without explanation. Her pained expression said enough. Maybe carrying it on my person will be some sort of penance. But I don't feel regret for what I did. Even if I was as selfish as I used to be—an open question, although one I'm not qualified to answer in full—this new world is about survival. And I didn't kill someone building hospitals for the poor.

I killed a man who ambushed travelers in the Lost Plains, stripped the lucky ones only of their vehicles and belongings. I don't believe in karma, but it's hard to conclude anything but the inevitable: Vlad Rose got what was coming. A murderous existence usually ends with the knife pointed the wrong way.

"They're getting lazy," Jana says, shielding her eyes from the glow of high beams as she surveys her people.

"Everyone's tired."

"We didn't survive by doing this shit." She walks off, leaving me alone. I shrug and turn my attention toward the empty way station. This one is a strange beast—it's a fifteen story building surrounded by nothing but empty road and frozen grass.

A nano-builder bot must've built this tiny skyscraper. It looks funny, like a giant accidentally dropped it in the landscape. The gate is open, so I walk through. I crane my head to look at the abandoned sniper's nest.

Two of them, in fact, framing the gate.

Years ago, waltzing through the gate would've been impossible. It's well-fortified enough to hold off attackers for days. But nothing stops me as I walk toward the entrance and wait for the motion sensing mechanism to let me in.

The sliding doors don't open, and I'm left staring at

my reflection. It's the first time I've seen myself since HIVE. I don't remember if I was better looking in the simulation. Probably. Three years and a load of shit have worn on my features. My black hair is longer, the ragged tips frosted by ashen dust.

"Who are you, Luke?" I say to the man I've become. I don't have an answer. The hardest man to know is yourself.

Then I rear back and send my boot through the reflection, shattering the glass. I brush away the jagged edges and step inside. The carpet smells fresh. Whoever ran this place was a neat freak. Not a bad place to catch a few winks, maybe even take a shower. A week ago, this would've been like an oasis. The bone-crushing weariness of those first few days out of HIVE were almost unbearable. But a man finds that he can bear almost anything, so long as he has enough time to adapt.

I'm still tired—it's just that I've become better at handling it. And I don't want to stay at this way station any longer than necessary. I walk over the tan carpet in the lobby, approaching the desk. It's faux-cherry and granite. From afar, it looks real, but up close you see the truth. I brush my hand over the clean surface. No dust.

It's only been a few days since the Remnants abandoned the way stations, throwing their lot in with either Jana or Mirko. Not beyond the realm of possibility that this little high-rise hasn't been reclaimed by nature, yet.

Clattering footsteps draw my attention to a dimly lit corner of the lobby.

"Hello?" I call into the darkness. No response. I reach for the rifle hanging off my back.

"Wouldn't do that," a craggy voice replies. A warning shot flies into the ceiling, and I dive behind the desk.

I take my hand off the rifle and peer into the black. "Who's there?" I can't see the glow of radioactive eyes, which means that the current proprietor of this establishment isn't a member of the Remnants.

"No one at all." I hear movement, then nothing. An elevator chimes, and I wait for an army to rush out. But no one comes.

My heart pounds as I race outside. The cold whips against my face. A light on the top floor comes on, and I hear a hush pass over the Remnants' makeshift camp a few hundred yards away.

At least this isn't a hallucination. I reach for my rifle and stare down the scope, trying to get a better look at the top floor. It's a penthouse, seamless glass—which is a funny perk, given the view—but no one seems to be present.

Jana appears behind me, her own rifle clattering. "You do that?"

"Why would I do that," I say. "To fuck with you?"

"Could be Circle," Jana says, still not quite adjusting to the reality of the New Allied States.

"It's the NAS, now," I say.

"This is what happens when you get lazy."

"I talked with…" I'm not sure if the indistinct voice was a him or her. "A single person. Probably not working with Blackstone."

Jana brings her head down from her own rifle scope and punches me in the arm. "You could lead with that."

I do a final scan with my rifle, but still see no sign of human movement on the top floor. It's sleight of hand—pure distraction.

"We're not gonna find anything," I say. "We can't stay."

"Everyone's exhausted," Jana says. "The black ice, the roads…"

"You don't need to explain," I say. "Just like I don't need to explain why staying here is a bad idea."

"It hasn't been abandoned long," Jana says. "Who could be inside?"

"I don't know." I don't want to find out, more importantly. But she has a point: pushing the Remnants further could result in mutiny, shattering whatever tenuous trust they have in Jana. It's already midnight, and we need supplies. A thousand people don't feed themselves.

I rub feeling into my cheeks with my gloved hands. "What's the worst case scenario?"

"You're the one who actually saw them."

"I didn't see anything." I look up at the sky, toward the glowing penthouse. My heart skips a beat when I squint into the starless night. "Up there."

"I already looked."

"Maybe we weren't looking for the right thing." I jab my finger at the top of the high-rise. "You see?"

Jana begrudgingly follows my finger, using her rifle scope as a visual aid. Then she lowers it slowly, a low murmur of assent rumbling in her throat. "Goddamn."

"Satellite dish," I say. "You know what that means."

"It's a longshot."

"We need to know who's chasing us," I say. "And where the NAS is headed. We're flying blind." I kick the dirt and adjust my rifle strap. Looking over my shoulder, I can sense a nervous thrum from the camp. "This is a chance to prove you're a leader."

"By flying blind?"

"Shows them you're not afraid," I say. "That we can actually win a battle."

"Now's not the time, Luke. We're weak, we're tired—"

"Consider it a bonding experience," I say, walking toward the gates. I'm not sure where this sudden burst of insane courage has come from, considering that ten minutes ago I was ready to tear ass across the plains. But Jana's right about one thing: you can't spend all your time running.

And if I can get any intel at all on what Blackstone's end game is, that can only help. Flying blind, it's only a matter of time before I'm dead anyway. I walk through the gates again, heading toward the broken entrance.

I hear boots pad across the frozen ground, and I crack a smile.

"No backup?"

"You're the one talking about morale," Jana says. She slides a clip into her rifle and checks the chamber. "Sounds like there's only one in here."

"So what were you so afraid of?"

Jana shakes her head and gives me a sad look. "The ambush. Whole place could be rigged to blow. Maybe there's a drone strike painted on this position."

"You've got a creative imagination," I say.

"Hell of a New Year's Eve, huh," Jana says. The glass crinkles as I step back into the lobby. The elevator is still open.

"Just let me know when the ball drops," I say as we enter the car.

"Why's that?"

"You know why," I say with a wink.

I'm not sure she gets it.

But I'll definitely kiss her if we're about to die.

14 | PENTHOUSE

THE ELEVATOR GRINDS to a halt. A flickering touchscreen in the corner indicates we're on the twelfth floor.

"Should've taken the stairs." I tap the plastic with my knuckle, but the screen doesn't respond. Above us, the pulleys and gears moan.

"Our friend must've blocked the shaft," Jana says, pointing at the ceiling. "Could drop hot oil on us, if they wanted. I've heard about this happening."

I glance at the tiles. There are no holes prepared for medieval style defensive measures. Still, the fact remains, we're stuck hanging over a hundred feet off the ground. The elevator continues to push upwards, fighting its way through the blockade.

Pressing the button for the lobby, I discover that the car won't reverse its direction mid-trip.

I grind my teeth and listen to the loud scraping. "That can't be good."

"Incredible assessment."

"Help me with the door," I say, gesturing toward the tiny crack. "You got something we can use?"

"I packed a crowbar specifically for this."

"You're the one who said this is a common occurrence." I try to snake my fingertips into the crevice, but it's too narrow to gain purchase. My sweaty fingers just slip over the brass finish. Above, the elevator bangs against a large obstacle, causing the entire cab to sway and shake. I'm sent against the wall as the interior lights flicker.

Then the touchscreen goes out, plunging the cab into darkness. But I can still see Jana's eyes glowing dimly in the black.

"You know," I say, "if the military was trying to build the ultimate soldier, they did a shit job with stealth."

"I'll take it up with my creator," Jana says. Don't know if she's talking about Vlad, or whoever helmed the project. But I drop the line of conversation, seeing as how it's not pertinent to our immediate survival. Our surroundings shake again, and my head bounces lightly off the padded wall.

"You can see, though," I say, reaching out into the blackness.

"Same as before," she says. "Stuck in purgatory."

"Try this." I reach into my waistband and extract the sharp blade from its scabbard. Trusting that she can indeed see in the darkness, I hold it out. My hand hangs in the empty space for a few seconds. Then I feel her take the knife with a sigh. In a world of drones, potentially super-human artificial intelligence and incredible virtual realities, a technology over 10,000-years-old keeps saving my ass.

The blade scratches against the metal with a spine-tingling dissonance before Jana manages to wedge it between the doors. I hear her massage it back and forth, using the knife as a lever.

"Working?"

"Come here." Her arm shoots out in the darkness and

pulls me over. I feel her hand guide mine toward the right area. "Pull when I do." I can tell that the doors are ajar. How far is anyone's guess.

"Are we on a floor?"

"Close enough," she says. "Pull."

All the muscles in my arms fire at once as I lean backwards. The doors groan and heave, fighting our manual labor. But they open. To where, I can't tell. Everything is still black. I hear Jana move, what sounds like a jump.

"Your turn," she says.

"I can't see shit."

"Just jump and I'll make sure land okay."

"I don't even know if I'm facing the right way." Above, a cable snaps, and the elevator lurches, throwing me against the side. Even with the padding, it knocks the wind out of me.

"It's about to fall," Jana says, her tone surprisingly cool. "Let's go, Luke."

On my hands and knees, I start crawling toward what I think is the door. I butt up against the back of the elevator as it sways precariously. The remaining steel cables unravel with an ominous hiss.

I reorient myself toward the front and stagger to my feet, taking careful steps. It's odd, because this blackness before me is the same as the rest. Except it's not—because a few steps too far, and I'll plummet to my death.

"Now," Jana says. "Jump now."

The elevator rocks and shakes.

The final cable snaps.

And I jump into the ether, relying on nothing but trust and faith.

*

NOT SURE WHAT I was expecting, but the slight drop throws me off. I crash into Jana and we tumble to the ground. We fall against the wall, drywall crumbling around us. The elevator car crashes to the ground, shaking the entire building.

I'm breathing heavily, still disoriented in the darkness. "Get off," Jana says.

Low wattage lights burst on, the dim orange glow feeling like a searchlight. I roll onto the plush carpet. My eyes adjust after a couple minutes. There's a big sign with *12* etched into the metal. It sits next to the empty elevator shaft.

Jana checks herself for scrapes and bruises. Apparently satisfied that everything is in order, she does a quick scan of the hall.

Before I can comment, the voice from downstairs crackles over the intercom. "Hello again."

Jana and I share a glance. Her face tattoo crinkles as the gears inside her mind turn. The tiniest sound of a camera focusing draws my attention above the sign. A red light blinks as the lens stares at me.

I reach over to rip it off the wall, but a racking cough makes me stop. When it's done coughing, the intercom voice says, "It's been too long, Luke. Didn't recognize you downstairs, old buddy."

"You know this asshole?" Jana says.

I shake my head, unable to place the voice. "How do you know my name?"

"You don't remember?" More coughs. The camera

zooms in closer, to what I imagine is right up on my face. "What'd you tell this broad to get her eating out of your hand?"

"He told me *nothing*," Jana says, her voice heavy with electric tension. "I'm the one in charge."

"Sure you are honey," the voice says. "That's what they all said."

"So you don't like me very much," I say. "That's fine."

"On the contrary, Luke," the voice says. "I'm your best friend."

Everything clicks together. "Sid?" He sounds nothing like he used to. Gave him shit all the time about his high-pitched voice. Now it sounds like he's picked up a ten-packs-a-day habit and started gargling battery acid. "You almost killed us, you son of a bitch."

There's a pause, punctuated by thin, gravelly laugh. "Can't be too careful, Luke. Didn't recognize you, and you brought the cavalry."

"Where are you?"

"Fourteenth floor," Sid says, coughing violently. "Leave the woman."

"I'm not staying here," Jana says.

"Take the stairs," Sid says, ignoring her. "I need some painkillers. You do that, honey, I'll tell your boyfriend everything he needs to know."

"I'm not your errand girl," Jana says. She racks the rifle and aims it at the camera. "How 'bout I just shoot you, instead?"

"I wired the bottom of the building," Sid says. "What I was doing when Luke interrupted me." There's a long cough. "You play by my terms, or you don't play at all. *Kaboom.*"

I raise my hands to indicate that we're backing off. "It's all cool, man. It's Luke. Remember?"

"I know who you are," he says with a bitter snort. "Don't think I'm not watching your ass, just 'cause you never fucked me over."

"I'll come alone," I say.

"End of the hall," Sid says. The intercom shuts off, but I'm sure he's still listening and watching. I nod toward Jana. She's reticent to come over, as if resisting me will prove that she's the lead. But right now we're playing by someone else's rules.

With more emphasis, I jerk my thumb toward the stairwell. She walks over with a sullen expression. As she passes, I whisper, "I know Sid. Get him the meds and he'll play ball."

"If he blows up this building—"

"And move your people back, okay," I say. "Get Evelyn to help."

Jana doesn't nod, but she does head toward the stairwell. I walk down the hall, in the opposite direction.

Hopefully fourteen is my lucky number.

*

FOUR KNOCKS, SPACED just so. Our old secret signal, from when we were young and believed stupid shit like that was cool.

"It's unlocked," Sid calls. I try the knob to the apartment and step inside. It's dark, but not pitch black. Not quite a penthouse, but on the rung directly below. A vast, loft-like space stretches out. One room, sections merging together seamlessly. Faux aged brick, leather furniture.

I spot movement in the kitchen, behind the stainless steel island. Sid limps into view, carrying a drink.

"I'm all out," he says with a warped grin. "Otherwise I'd offer you one."

I don't answer. I'm too busy taking stock of what my old friend has become. The skin is tight around his cheeks, a sickly shade of grayish white. His shirt is spattered with blood, his eyes sunken deep inside his skull. Once thick black hair has turned into just a few wisps.

He was never a big guy, which is why we got along. Kind of cut from the same mold—had to talk fast, move quick, stay out of the direct line of fire. But now, he can't weigh more than a hundred pounds.

"I know, I know," Sid says. "I'm still a handsome son of a bitch."

Only ten feet separate us, but it's more like an entire lifetime. At one point, our paths ran parallel. But now, after three years, those roads have diverged in wild fashion. I spot Ramses panting in the corner, whining.

However bad these hallucinations are, they're a gift compared to whatever happened to Sid.

Eventually, I gather the wherewithal to move across the room. Afraid that I'll crush him with a hug, and not eager to feel his feeble bones against mine, I offer him a handshake.

"All business," Sid says. "Or maybe we grew up, right buddy?" He still takes my hand and gives it a weak shake.

"Slick said you all died. The whole crew."

"So you seen Slick?" Sid's eyes get a little fire in them

for a moment. He drains the rest of his beverage—vodka, judging from the rubbing alcohol aroma. "That what he told you, huh?"

"Yeah."

"Guess that's what you can expect from a liar." Sid staggers around the island and takes the bottle. "See, I was lying when you came in."

He hands me the cheap vodka, and I take a swig. "We all had a lot of practice."

"You wanna know what Slick did?"

"You wanna tell me?" I pass the bottle back, studying his expression.

"I'm not a mark," Sid says. "Look around. There's nothing of value. You don't have to play that shit that with me." He can barely raise his hand above his chest. I'm sure being half-wasted on shitty liquor isn't helping, but it's clear he doesn't have much time left.

"Old habits," I say. "Make 'em feel comfortable. Like your friend. Isn't that what Slick used to say?"

"One of his rules," Sid says with a bitter laugh. "Guess that list didn't include helping us escape."

I wait until he's ready to share. Then Sid says, "We were across town, running a grift. Trying to steal a shipment of HoloBands off a truck. Planned this shit for weeks. Me, Jay, Manny, a few of the others, some hired guns, we were about to do it. Radio silence the whole time, so that none of the guards could pick up our frequencies. That's when it happened."

"What happened?"

"The damn quake." Sid spits on the ground. "He could've told us. Early warning systems told everyone with a HoloBand about it." He takes a long swig. "But we didn't have them installed, and he didn't radio to warn us. That fifteen minutes allowed his ass to get out. Far enough to find shelter, at least."

"How do you know Slick boned you guys?"

"Because Mariah was with him," Sid says. He laughs when he sees my expression. "Yeah, they were back together."

"Jesus."

"And she warned us a couple minutes before. But by that time, we were fucked. The others died in the quake. They were lucky." Sid tosses the bottle across the room, and it breaks with a loud crack. "We heard him shoot Mariah for warning us. Potentially alerting the Circle and all that."

Folding his hand into a pistol shape, he cocks the imaginary trigger, lines up the shot, and fires into the dim loft.

I stroke my chin, unsure what to say. Slick wasn't a good Samaritan, but damn.

"Yeah, I guess your daddy wasn't all you thought he was," Sid says.

"He wasn't my father."

"Might as well have been," Sid says.

"That all you have to tell me?"

"Aw, hell, Stokes," Sid says. "You're not gonna ask me about my cough? How the hell I got here?"

"I don't really care," I say, dropping any pretense. "You're an asshole, just like you were before."

"That's why we were such good friends." The words are slurred and incoherent. "The ash, it gets in your lungs. Becomes part of you. Gums you up from the inside."

"Sad story." A light blinks over the stove, indicating that someone has buzzed up to the apartment. "Your delivery's here."

Sid stumbles over to the intercom and says, "Leave it where you came in."

I hear Jana say, "I'm coming up."

"You do that, bitch, and I light this entire place up."

There's a sigh, but Jana says, "Okay."

When Sid hobbles over to me, he gives me a look. "Why you still here?"

"You were gonna tell me something important." I want to reach out and slug him. But that would be pathetic for us both. Him telling me about Slick served no purpose other than to throw my mind off. That's the problem when you get two con artists in the same room. They're trying to mind-fuck the other guy so hard that, eventually, they assure each other's destruction.

I knew Slick was a prick, a liar, an opportunist. Then again, if I make it out of here, that piece of information does serve one purpose: Slick's even more dangerous than I thought. Maybe Blackstone isn't my main enemy.

"Maybe I was just shittin' you."

"Nah." I look him straight in his dead eyes. "You were gonna tell me everything I need to know, if I recall. I already knew Slick's a piece of shit. Lot has happened in the past three years."

He coughs, bringing his shirt up to his mouth to catch the bloody phlegm.

"You grab the meds, I got something to tell you."

"You're gonna have to give me more than that."

"How about this," Sid says with a conspiratorial grin. "Out west, there's a new faction. And they might just save your new broad's ass."

I try to read him, but in the dim light, his body fading, three years and a lifetime between us, I can't tell if he's full of shit.

Still, I say, "I'll get the pills."

"Good man," Sid says as I head toward the door.

At least we both know that's a lie.

15 | SATELLITE

"YOU GAVE HIM the pills before he gave you the information?" Jana checks Sid's pulse again, but it's pointless. He's been dead for the past half hour, and he's not coming back. A foamy froth of spittle is caked around his pale lips. "How dumb are you?"

"He didn't know anything else." That's what I decided when I was walking down the stairs to get the meds from Jana. I could burn a lot of time having a circle jerk with an old friend for a few hours, or I could get straight to it. Death was a mercy. No need to prolong the inevitable.

When I became so concerned about the welfare of others, I'm not sure. Normally, that would be considered a sign of growth. But in this world, it's the opposite of evolution—maladaptive to the ruthless, lawless environment in which I'm trying to survive.

"Oh, as long as you say so." Jana kicks the empty plastic bottle across the room. It bounces off the faux-weathered brick with an empty echo. "Tell me he shut off the explosives."

"That was a bluff," I say. "Look at him. He could barely lift a bottle to his mouth." At least, I'm about ninety percent sure he was full of shit. But it wasn't like I could get a straight answer from him while he was still breathing, anyway.

"Lot of conclusions you're drawing, here. You should've been a scientist."

"Look at it this way."

"What way?"

"We get a nice fireworks show if he rigged the place to blow," I say. "Perfect for that kiss."

"Do you always think with your dick?"

"Only when there are pretty girls around."

She flushes and plays with her hair. "I'm not going on your list, Luke."

"Okay," I say with a nonplussed shrug.

"What does *that* mean?"

"You want to talk about what I didn't do, or what I *did* do?" I say. "Because Sid did tell me one thing before I handed everything over."

"So you're not a complete idiot."

"He told me the satellite up on the roof works," I say. "And he's been getting clear feeds recently, directly from the Origin Point."

"Blackstone's speeches?"

"You got it."

Jana runs her boot over the hardwood, playing with a loose plank. It wobbles as she adjusts her weight.

"You believe him about this other faction?"

I glance down at Sid. He looks about as alive as he did when he was actually breathing. Can you trust a dead man? There's no good answer. Conventional wisdom would say that you can, simply because he has no reason to lie. But what happens when a habit has been woven into the very fabric of his being? Leopards, I'm told, have a hell of a time changing their spots.

"There's gotta be a few survivors." I purse my lips together and choose my next words carefully. "But I guess that depends on your definition of *survive*."

"So you think they're like him?"

"I think we should keep our eyes open," I say. "Because whoever's living out in the Gray Desert might have a nasty bite."

Jana nods. I'm speaking a hopeless, hyper-vigilant language she understands. "I'm going up to the roof. You coming with?"

"Just tell me what that prick Blackstone has to say."

"You gonna do anything with your friend?"

I reach over and close Sid's blank eyes. "Haven't decided."

Jana leaves me without another word.

*

"Hey." An arm grabs my shoulder. Instinctively, I reach toward my waistband. A sharp pain goes through my wrist, and I drop the knife on the ground. "It's me, moron."

I shake free of Jana's grip. My back is stiff from falling asleep against the wall. The sun is rising outside.

"How long have I been out?"

"Awhile," Jana says. "I think we should stay here for a couple days."

I scan her eyes for a reason, but find nothing. "You hear anything on the radio?"

She shakes her head. "I want to keep trying, though."

"We can't stay here."

"It's a new day," Jana says. "A new year. Gotta relax for a day or two. Morale."

"It's a bad idea."

"Duly noted," Jana says. "I'm thinking about staying longer."

"*What*?"

"Fifteen floors, clear line of sight." She paces back and forth, her footsteps heavy. "There's a reason we made it a way station. And it's far enough from the Circle—"

"New Allied States," I say. "Or did you forget that everyone's gonna be coming after us?"

"You don't know that," Jana says. She points at Sid's stiff body. "He survived out here like that."

"I'm telling you—"

"I heard you. And I'm in charge."

That ends the conversation. I watch her disappear from the loft. She slams the door shut behind her. I shake my head and stare at the tall ceiling. Even without any intel or notion about what Blackstone and his minions are up to, I know, deep in my bones, that this is a bad idea.

But if there's a faction in the Gray Desert, I'll need the full strength of Jana's tiny army to advance.

Which means, for now, I'll need to follow the leader.

16 | JANUARY FROST

IF I IGNORE the nagging sense of dread, the fifteen-story building I've been calling home for the past three weeks is almost pleasant. Food is beginning to run out, but the rest, clean water and actual heat have restored morale amongst the Rems.

I spend most of my days on the roof, listening in quiet hope that the sky will align in such a way that I'll get a snippet of a broadcast. Never have I wanted to hear Old Silver Fox's voice so bad. But nothing comes, no matter how many hours I spend in the sub-zero frost alone.

None of the Rems join me. They're caught in a whirlwind of hope, blind to reality. I've heard mentions of spring, how they'll plant crops. Ways to build up the defenses, increase the yield of the solar panels lining the roof so that we won't have to ration energy.

It's a nice enough fantasy.

I peer through my rifle scope, out at the empty plains. Nothing moves on the frozen tundra. Nothing ever moves. And that's what scares me so damn much.

I rub the frost clinging to the fine hair at my temples.

I've gotten used to the cold. It's become a friend, a familiar reminder that, despite the peaceful interlude, the world remains harsh and unforgiving.

Footsteps patter across the icy roof, and I wheel around, rifle aimed at the sound.

"Don't shoot," Evelyn says. "It's just me." She holds up a stainless steel mug of coffee. "Figured you could use a drink."

She's the only one who comes up here. Sometimes she'll sit near the edge, where the railing has fallen away, eyes closed. Meditating on what, I don't know. But I get the impression that, she, like me, is trying to face reality: that we are all living on the edge of a razor blade, about to topple off.

"What's the word from downstairs?"

"They're tired," Evelyn says. "This is like paradise."

I sip from the hot mug, grimacing as I taste the synthetic grounds. "Some paradise."

"Everything is relative."

"How Zen."

"See anything new today?"

"Just waiting," I say, watching her deep brown eyes scan the barren plains. "Same as yesterday."

"Who's Zen, now?" Evelyn tosses her long blonde hair and then walks to her corner of the roof. I watch her settle in before I resume fiddling with the dish. Despite all evidence to the contrary, if I can get the angle *just* right, it'll fix everything. Suddenly, answers will descend from the sky.

And we'll be saved.

It's a fanciful wish. But I can see why the Lionhearted are so damn eager to place all their eggs in the God basket.

I fiddle with the small radio jerry-rigged to the satellite dish. But I still get no signal. Fucking Sid. I sigh and sip the coffee. If this qualifies as paradise, I don't want to know what hell looks like. If it's worse than the Gunpowder Hills, I'd prefer not to see it in this lifetime.

"Someone's coming," Evelyn says from across the roof. I look past the rows of solar panels. Her blonde hair flutters over the broken railing.

"The spirits tell you that?"

"The ground shaking told me that," Evelyn says. "It's physics."

"I can't feel anything."

Her eyes open a sliver, the brown peeking out. Her silent gaze implores me to *look*, to feel. I bring my rifle scope up to my eye and scan the horizon. Far off, maybe two or three miles, I spot a slight disturbance in the frozen soil. What looks like a fog, but is, upon closer inspection, the breath of men tramping across the plains.

"Holy shit." I do a double-take to make sure. "You see that?"

"You're not hallucinating," Evelyn says. "Unless we both are."

"Comforting," I say. I look down at the useless satellite dish. "You just gonna sit there?"

"You can't let circumstance interrupt who you are."

I have no fucking idea what that means. My senses are on full-tilt high-alert. This is what I was so damn worried about—and now there's an army at our doorstep.

"I gotta warn Jana."

"Everything will be all right."

Evelyn stays in place, unperturbed by this development. I race off the roof, flinging the steel door open.

As I take the steps two at a time, I run down the options. Evacuating the Rems is going to be impossible. We're not prepared to escape. Everyone's guard is down.

That leaves only one option. I race into the fourteenth floor hallway, to the one working elevator.

"Come on, come on," I say, jabbing the button. Now, I swear I can feel the earth moving, too. But that's just paranoia. One thing's certain, though. In a few minutes, those footsteps will be trampling our faces, if we're not careful.

The elevator dings, and I dart inside. When I press the touchscreen button for the penthouse, a picture of a radio appears to indicate that it's connecting with the owner. No unauthorized access. It's just another annoying reminder of why I can't keep wasting my days here.

I want like hell to get out to the Gray Desert. For one thing, this damn dog Ramses follows me for about half my waking hours. But it's also a matter of inertia. Once our enemies become too powerful, stopping their advance will be impossible. They will simply roll over us, buoyed by the power of HIVE, superior numbers and a well-orchestrated plan.

Jana's voice comes over the elevator intercom. "Who's—oh, Luke." She doesn't sound pleased to see me. I haven't talked to her in a week, because she's been busy with preparations and such.

Preparations to stay.

"We got a problem," I say. "Look out your window."

"I'm busy, Luke," she says. Her council members chatter in the background. It's like the Remnants were never split in two. Same customs, same tribe, just smaller. Because things worked out so damn well the first time around.

Then again, habits are hard to shake. Ask Sid.

"There's an army at our door," I say. Then, I can't help myself. "Damnit, Jana, I told you this would happen."

The line hisses shut, and my request to go upstairs is denied. I smack my hand against the touchscreen. It comes back on, and Jana says, "Don't do that. Maintenance is a problem."

"Just listen to me."

"What do you think our preparations were for?" Jana says. "We're not fools."

"I don't understand."

"Go back to the roof and play your games," Jana says coolly. "Enjoy the show."

I punch the padded wall and step into the hall, seething. I want to scream and shout, kick down the door to the apartment that will be my home forever—or two more minutes. Fists clenched, I instead head back to the roof. The rifle bounces against my chest.

Like hell I'm going down without a fight.

Evelyn is still in the same place I left her. The army is close enough that I can see their ranks. Maybe five hundred strong. They're at the edge of where all the bikes and trucks are parked in the icy fields.

The first wave marches forward, and a series of explosions lights up the midday air. Fireballs erupt into the sky, bathing the windshields of the parked vehicles with ash. There are distant screams. Men try to retreat, but charges go off in the rear, too, boxing them in.

The bloodbath is absolute. In less than five minutes, there is little sign of the army other than the charred earth and a few struggling survivors in the blackened earth.

I look over incredulously at Evelyn, who still meditates in the breeze. The aroma of unspeakable things is carried on the wind, but she seems not to notice.

"How can you just sit there?"

"It's the only way I'll survive," Evelyn says.

"By ignoring everything?" A final explosive goes up as one of the remaining soldiers triggers a hidden mine buried in the soil. I peer through the scope, trying to identify just who came to attack. The uniforms bear a logo similar enough to the Circle's that I can only determine it's the New Allied States.

"Accept things the way they are," Evelyn says, with a certain sadness in her voice. "Accept the flow of life."

I kick the small radio off the roof, sending it hurtling to the ground below. With the crackle of flame and whistling wind, it barely makes a sound. But then, this is the world we live in. A few hundred lives didn't make much of a sound, either.

"I'm going down," I say.

Evelyn says nothing. When I look back, before I plunge into the stairwell, I see her staring at me. Searching for answers to the same question.

Is this all there is?

But finding none.

*

THERE ARE THREE survivors, all badly injured. One dies on the ground. The other two are shuttled into the high-rise, away from view. While I walk through the carnage, idly passing the flames, I find mementos.

Charred pictures. A rabbit foot that didn't bring luck. Tattered uniforms. No one looks like your enemy up close. The Remnants run through the wreckage, salvaging anything that's still intact.

I ask one of them, "There any other minefields I should know about?"

The man gives me an odd look and says, "Don't worry. They're all remote triggered."

Then he goes back to looting a half-torched corpse. He finds a gold wedding band and a wind-proof lighter, then moves on to the next unfortunate soul.

I wander out of the blast zone, unable to think straight. I trace the tracks of the men until I'm a couple miles away from our settlement. The tracks on the frozen ground are orderly, regimented. This alliance clearly has a well-trained force, although one not quite ready for guerilla tactics. But I suspect they'll adjust quickly. From the size of the squad, these were scouts. Which goes to show just how much stronger Blackstone is than the Rems.

I walk away from the tracks, finding an untouched patch of soil. The ice cracks when I sit down cross-legged. Cold seeps into my bones, but I barely feel it.

From here, I can still see our little high-rise in the middle of nothingness. Like the Earth in the middle of a bleak an empty universe.

Except this universe wants to kill us.

Ramses trots over and growls.

I reach over and pet his damp, wiry coat.

"I know, boy."

Today reminded me of one damn thing.
I gotta get to the Gray Desert.
Or part of me—all of me—is gonna die.

17 | NEW PROBLEMS

"I WAS THERE, Luke," Carina says, holding a hot cloth over my head as I shiver. The last two days, ever since I decided to try meditating in the middle of the frozen tundra, I've been sick as hell. The only plus has been that the hallucinations have stopped. "You didn't see what she did to those men."

I bat her hand away and try to focus on her eyes. They're not quite as soulful a brown as Evelyn's. Little golden flecks at the edges give a playful, hopeful quality. Long lashes bring out a certain sensuality that she's probably embarrassed about.

She catches me staring and she looks away. Plays with the empty silver chain around her neck. A placeholder for a cross in a world that doesn't allow anyone to wear one. Her high cheekbones tense when she touches my forehead. "You're still burning up."

"Evelyn told me something funny the other day."

"We talk a lot," Carina says. "She knows so much about the world. Did you know that—"

"I slept with her, you know," I say.

"I know," she says in a small voice. "I think she loves you too."

A weird sensation rushes through my chest. One I'd like to chalk up to whatever illness I contracted by being an idiot out on the plains, but simply can't. I'm torn between the con and the truth. *Keep it going*, a little voice whispers in my head. *She'll be useful later.*

Just keep the string going until everything's played out, and there's only enough rope left for the other person to hang themselves. That's the thing about cons. You never see the aftermath. You've already skipped out, on to the next one.

I compromise and keep my mouth shut while she adjusts the cloth on my head.

"You don't have anything stronger, do you?"

"Jana keeps the medicine," Carina says. "She's kind of scary."

"Tell me about it."

"I was telling you about it. You haven't been listening."

I smile at this little bit of fire from the woman Evelyn calls the church mouse. I saw it three years ago, when she told me she loved me and I deflected. Quick as it comes, it's gone.

"I'm a little sick here, in case you didn't notice."

"Sorry," Carina says.

"Why isn't Evelyn doing this?" She's the nurse, after all. Carina just scanned people at the gates, letting them into New Manhattan from the transcontinental Hyperloop.

"She's got a plan," Carina says in a clandestine whisper. She squeezes the rag a little too hard, and a stream of hot water drips into my eyes. I blink rapidly, too weak to wipe my own face.

"I need to sleep," I say in a faraway voice. Somewhere, I hear a dog growl. "Fuck you, Ramses."

"We have to get out of here," Carina says, and I shiver. Not because I'm cold or sick, but because I realize, in her fearful tone, that there's someone out there going through the same thing. "Can I show you something?"

"I'm tired."

"I need to show you, Luke. Down in the lobby. It's about the—visions."

Visions. That's a good euphemism. Ramses barks. "Okay."

"It's in the lobby."

"Carina…"

"I know, I know," she says. "I promise it's worth it."

I look at her. She's as scared as I am about losing my damn mind.

And about what this place will do to what's left of our humanity.

So I limp out the door and follow her to the elevator.

*

"No one else found these?" I say. We're in a side-room off the lobby, labeled Business Center, which I find amusing. I doubt any business ever took place in here, judging from the pristine gray carpets and untouched workstations.

Carina helps me to the end, where a large pod resides. It resembles an archaic version of the HIVE setup.

"You know the satellite doesn't work, right?"

She points along the left-hand edge of the pod's smooth surface. A tiny glass window, about three inches high, runs along the side. I see quarter-sized HoloBands inside.

"Demo units," Carina says. "It's for people on the fence about getting a HoloBand." She slides the glass away. "*Was*, I guess."

I look at the pod unit again, and walk around to the back. It has promotional information on the back, along with the Golden Nectar logo. It's strange that they needed a trial unit when GN had a monopoly on all things tech.

Then again, injecting something into the base of your neck does tend to raise objections.

When I return to the front, Carina is prepping what looks like a long syringe. The stainless steel has a surgical glint.

"What're you doing," I say, suddenly wary.

"You need to remember what it was like," Carina says. "In there."

"I'm good."

The golden flecks in her eyes flash hot. "No. You need to *remember*."

Before I can react, she sticks me with the needle. There's a tight feeling at the base of my neck.

"Goddamnit, Carina," I say. "I don't want to go back."

"You have to," she says, with a quiet strength. Then she pushes me into the pod and shuts the window. "Just settle into the back."

I begrudgingly have to admit that the interior is comfortable. Golden Nectar did their best to make the HoloBand tech as appealing as possible. I relax into the leather seat, even if I'm skeptical about this serving any purpose.

I'm not worried about the NAS tracking the HoloBand's signal—without satellite coverage, that won't be an issue. Which is the same reason I'm convinced I'll see nothing: this isn't even related to HIVE. It's like comparing a tricycle to a hover bike. Same basic idea, but not the same tech.

I look out at Carina, who is whispering a silent prayer.

Wires reach out from the chair, snaking into the back of my neck to connect with the trial HoloBand. I hear a scan booting up.

"Welcome, new user," a friendly female voice announces. "Are you interested in genetically printing your HoloBand, or the featured trial?"

I glare forward at the touchscreen, which encourages me to make a decision. Carina taps on the glass.

"Do the trial and select memory access," Carina says.

"Nothing's recorded," I say.

"It'll pull fragments and memories from your subconscious."

"I don't have amnesia," I say. The lights blink, trying to force me to choose. "I remember what happened."

"Not really," Carina says. "Trust me."

With a drawn out sigh, I reach forward and select featured trial.

"Excellent choice," the female voice says. "You have three options. HoloNet access—"

I reach out and tap the memory access button. This should be good.

"One moment, please," the female voice says. "Would you prefer the memories play on the screen, or for you to have a virtual experience? The HoloBand pod is capable of recreating sensations of weather, touch and smell."

That's new. Golden Nectar really pulled out all the stops for these units.

I stare out the tinted glass. My body hurts, and my mind is fuzzy. This is not what I want to be doing. But my caretaker has seen fit to bring me down here.

"What'd Jana think of this?"

"The Rems don't care about any of this tech," Carina says. "I don't think they care what happened to us."

Just like we don't really care what Damien Ford did to them. It's more a matter of *can't* care—without the visceral experience of betrayal being your own, it's impossible to be angry.

"Which option?" I say. "You're the boss."

"The virtual experience," Carina says. "It's not HIVE, but it's the closest thing we have."

As I press the button, I'm thinking about tricycles and hover bikes.

But when I remove my finger from the screen, everything disappears around me.

*

RAIN WHIPS DOWN in sheets from the gray sky. The Space Needle looms outside the car's tinted windows as we roll down the street.

Evelyn's driving, her fingers white from gripping the wheel so tightly.

"I can't believe you lost him," Evelyn says.

"It wasn't my fault."

"I told you not to walk Ramses without a leash," Evelyn says. "I fucking told you." The engine revs, and I'm afraid she'll crash.

"We'll find him," I say. "It'll be okay."

"It better."

I don't like the sound of that. It has shades of sleeping on the couch forever. I press my nose up against the glass, scanning the quiet suburban neighborhood for any sign of a hundred-pound dog. There's nothing.

"Look, maybe if you slowed down—"

"He went this way, Luke." Her voice is tight, like she's about to cry. I fiddle with the radio and she slaps my hand away. "Concentrate."

"He'll turn up."

"You said that already, and yet, here we are." Evelyn maneuvers the car down a cul-de-sac.

"*There*," I say. Up ahead, in someone's yard. My heart stops beating so damn fast. Crisis averted. Ramses is just rummaging around with a hamburger wrapper.

Evelyn slams on the brakes suddenly and pops out of the car. "Ramses!"

The dog perks his big, dumb ears up and looks for the familiar voice. When he rushes to greet Evelyn, he's stopped at the edge of the yard. A violent shock rolls through his body, and he whimpers.

I follow her out of the car, wondering what the hell is going on. Ramses wags his tail, but doesn't try to exit the yard again.

A man comes out of the two-story town home. Something about his appearance reminds me of someone I once knew. The rain drips off his thick glasses. It doesn't rustle his side part.

"Shock collar," he says with an easy smile. "For the dog. So he didn't run away."

He walks forward and pats Ramses. The dog whimpers slightly, clearly not a fan of his rescuer.

"Take that thing off my dog," Evelyn says. I think she's gonna leap off the sidewalk and strangle this guy, but instead she just stands there coiled like a rattlesnake.

"Of course," the man says. "Let me speak with your husband for a moment. Luke Stokes, right?"

"How'd you know my name?" I say.

"You're famous," he says. There's a long pause, then he adds, "I'm kidding. The dog's collar. I was about to call you when you arrived."

The man takes me by the triceps and leads me down the sidewalk. Evelyn doesn't follow.

"If you want a reward, I got some money in the car."

"No, nothing like that, Stokes," he says like an old friend. "How are you doing?"

"I'm okay," I say, uncomfortable now. "Thanks for saving my dog."

"You feeling okay, Stokes?"

"Look, man, I don't know you—"

"Of course," the man says with an easy smile. He wipes the rain from his glasses. When he looks at me without them, it's almost like he sees better. "It's just, a man doesn't lose his dog without something troubling him."

"Everything's fine," I say. "Look, Mister—"

"Vegas," the man says. "Kid Vegas."

"Yeah, whatever," I say. "I need to go."

He doesn't try to stop me as I hurry away. Evelyn's removed Ramses' collar and has him in the car. I get in the passenger seat.

"Floor it."

"That guy creeps me out," she says.

I don't answer. Wet dog permeates the air. The man's eyes follow us all the way up the cul-de-sac. Once we're out of sight, I shiver.

For some reason, I get the impression that this Vegas fellow has been watching us the whole time.

*

I COME BACK to reality with a start. My body aches worse than when I entered.

"Get me out," I yell, banging against the side of the pod. Carina hurries to lift it up and help me out.

"What'd you see?"

"I saw that son of a bitch Vegas," I say. "He was watching us the whole time in HIVE."

"I know."

I look at Carina as we push through the door out of the business center. "What'd he do to you?"

"Sat in the back of the church," Carina says. "Asked me about you."

"We gotta stop the NAS," I say, leaning against her.

"We have to stop *him*," she says. "*He* did this."

I think back to the car crash in the jewelry store. A few more steps, a knife to the ribs to finish the job—it would've been so easy. Most things, in retrospect, are.

"I told you," Carina says. "We leave as soon as you're well. Evelyn has a plan."

When we get to the elevator, I collapse inside.

*

ANOTHER THREE DAYS, and I can finally stand.

Carina helps me into my jeans. "I washed your shirt."

"Thanks," I say, wincing as I tug it over my head. Every muscle is heavy with the sort of infinite soreness that you're sure will never disappear. I stifle a small cough. She reaches out to help me with the right sleeve. "*I* got it."

"Okay," Carina says. The apartment door opens, and we both jump slightly. We share a brief understanding glance, how stressful it is to have your senses continually betray you. Evelyn comes inside the loft and hurriedly shuts the door. Frost clings to her golden hair, which is frozen stiff.

"Glad you're awake," Evelyn says. "There's a lot to talk about."

"Apparently you've been busy."

"Taking up the mantle of a hero is never easy," Evelyn says.

I smirk and walk toward the kitchen. It takes both hands to get a mug out of the cabinet.

"If you're making a run for it, I think you'll have to carry me," I say.

"She's digging in, Luke," Carina says. She shuffles over to help me with the coffee. I give her a small nod of thanks and allow her to pour the cup. "She wants to stay."

"Ev?"

Evelyn laughs from across the room. "No. Jana Rose. Your new flame."

I wince and rub my temple. "You guys need to let this shit go. You're all grown-ups."

"Believe me, you're not that much of a catch." The Zen-ness from the day of the rooftop attack is gone. Whatever's transpired while I've been sick has clearly rattled Evelyn in a way that a series of massive explosions couldn't.

"Someone just tell me what's going on." The cup trembles so much when I try to lift it that I'm afraid I'm going to drop it. So I pretend I'm waiting for it to cool. "Why you two have been making plans and showing me old memories and shit."

"Jana tortured the survivors," Evelyn said. "We were there. I had to—I had to…"

Carina leans toward me, her hair brushing against my cheek. "She had to keep them alive long enough to tell Jana everything."

The coffee doesn't seem all that appetizing. I lean against the counter and say, "Shit."

"Yeah, shit," Evelyn says. "No wonder everyone hates the Rems."

I do recall that, when I saved Jana from execution, it was her people who had tried to ambush us our party first. Brutality runs deep within their culture. Perhaps the reason they survived this long.

I glance between my two cohorts. They, like me, are apparently hoping there's another way.

"Did the soldiers say anything?"

Evelyn rubs her hands together and closes her eyes. "A lot of things."

"Care to elaborate?"

"Not really."

"That wasn't really a question," I say.

"Jesus Christ, Luke," Evelyn says, pushing over a lamp. I feel Carina's nails dig into my arm—whether it's from a lack of reverence for the savior, or because Evelyn blowing her stack is rarer than seeing a wooly mammoth is hard to tell. "She dug a man's eye out with her bare hands."

She holds two curled fingers out, and then violently yanks them through the air.

"I get the picture," I say.

"You can't get it. You weren't there."

"Someone's gotta fill me in on what happened."

They take turns detailing Jana's torture tactics and the information derived from her innovative methods. When one gets tired of recounting the relentlessness brutality, the other takes over. It's hard to tell if the story is long, or simply exhausting, but by the end of their summary, my mind is torn in six different directions.

Ramses sits down and whines in the corner, then disappears into the ether as the story comes to its grim conclusion.

"So that's why we're leaving. Tomorrow," Evelyn says with final emphasis. Carina nods, but doesn't say anything, like she's afraid any chance of me loving her will go away if I don't agree.

"Wonderful. You got a plan?"

Evelyn just says, "Meet us by the vehicles at seven tomorrow morning."

Then they both leave me alone without explaining further.

*

IT'S A LONG night. I can only imagine what it's been like for the two of them. Evelyn saw some savage things as a member of the Ashes of the Fall. Carina, well, probably not. But anything they'd experienced pales in comparison to being complicit with torture.

Not that they had a choice. You want to stay in paradise, you gotta play by the rules.

It went a little something like this: The leaders of the factions—Chancellor Blackstone, President Alfred "Slick" Knute, and Reverend Amelia Daniels—had quickly agreed that the best path to rebuilding was to first put down the Remnants. The first soldier broke quickly, told Jana that the rest of the Remnants—the ones under Mirko's rule—had been annihilated by the NAS force. Then the NAS had cut through the way stations next, systematically capturing them one-by-one.

Sieging the Gunpowder Hills had cost them a couple weeks, but the victory, ultimately, had been absolute. All the Remnants had been put to death.

After learning that, Jana had killed the first man in a fit of rage. His counterpart, however, had not been so fortunate. For over three days he had been kept alive, Evelyn's nursing skills betraying her horribly. Each time the man appeared ready to die, Jana ordered him revived. Carina was allowed reprieve from this prolonged torture to care for me.

Eventually, however, all the news I couldn't get from the satellite spilled from this soldier's lips: how a new NAS Inner Circle had formed, this time with a mission of transparency and trust. Blackstone, Kid Vegas and Olivia were the representatives from the Circle. Other than the leaders from the other two factions, he didn't know the names of the other members.

The plan to conquer was simple: scrub the Remnants from the Lost Plains by the end of February. Then a push into the Gray Desert, particularly a spot about a hundred miles south of Seattle, near I5. Details weren't given to the soldiers about why this location was important.

But a scout party had already been sent to comb through the wreckage. Pain surges through my skull when I consider that Blackstone and Kid might already have the fail-safe.

Oh, and about HIVE—the man was kind enough to relay that it was operational, complete with a new offer. Those ineligible for armed service could upload their consciousness into the cloud, freeing them of their earthly shackles. The cost was entirely free, with prime placement in the system given on a first-come, first-serve basis. Response had been overwhelming. Over a quarter of the population had already consigned themselves to a virtual existence.

Well, there was one particularly compelling side note—those who uploaded their consciousness to the HIVE servers were guaranteed to live forever. So long as the servers stay on, they'll live in complete and ignorant bliss.

I hear Ramses growl somewhere in the room. An image of the Space Needle—first pristine, then cracked—pops across my closed eyes. The NAS probably didn't explain the side effects. Then again, if you're never removed from HIVE, maybe these hallucinations don't affect you.

All the new intel threatens to short-circuit my brain, until I realize it leads to the same conclusion I've always had: I need to get to Matt's fail-safe in the ruins of the Gray Desert. A cure for my hallucinations and a bullet in Blackstone's head wouldn't be bad bonuses.

But first, I gotta reach the HIVE fail-safe. Because as it expands and grows in consciousness, time runs out. And if the NAS reaches Matt's fail-safe, we're all very screwed. That type of power cannot be wielded by men like Blackstone or Slick.

I curl up, making sure my alarm is set for tomorrow.

Whatever the plan is, one thing's certain.

After seven, nothing will ever quite be the same.

18 | ANCIENT TRUCKS

I HOBBLE OUT of the high-rise into the gray morning light. After a final glance back at the shattered entrance, I put my head down to guard against the stiff wind. I'm not fully recovered, but escape plans don't wait for perfect circumstances.

And staying here, I'll die. If not by a bullet, in a very real, yet slightly less tangible way. Maybe I'm already dying because of this place and what I've seen. We all know that illness isn't caused by cold. Perhaps it's guilt.

The ground crinkles beneath my boots as I trek through the fresh snowfall. There's two pairs of recent tracks leading toward the vehicles parked a couple hundred yards outside the way station's gates. The sun fights against the white-gray horizon. It's too early in the day to know if its efforts will prove futile.

A low whistle catches my attention near the first row of dirt bikes.

"Over here," Evelyn calls. Her soft voice carries on the empty plains so loudly that it might as well be an air horn. I weave in and out of the bikes and head toward the diesel cargo trucks. After the third row, I find her and Carina leaning up against a pickup.

"What's the plan?"

"There's food in the back," Evelyn says. "We've been stealing it for the past few days."

Carina nods—or maybe it's just a shiver from the bone-numbing cold.

"You got the keys?"

"That's where you can help," Evelyn says. "You know how to hot-wire a truck, right?"

I give her a slightly offended look. "*Me?*"

"You can, right?" Anxiety flashes over Evelyn's face. If this was her plan, I don't know why she couldn't have told me yesterday. So I let her simmer for a little while.

Then I say, "Yeah, I can handle it."

"Asshole."

I look at Carina, but her eyes are shut tightly. "It's gonna be all right." I touch her arm, but she just shakes. Whatever she's seeing, hopefully we can find a cure for that in the west.

Using the knife and one of Evelyn's bobby pins, I manage to pick the truck's driver-side lock. An alarm begins to howl.

"Why didn't you steal the keys?" I yell over the din, beckoning for them to climb in before me. "I could've just stolen the fucking keys."

"You were about to die until yesterday," Evelyn says, helping Carina over the gear shift in the center of the front seat. "Didn't think you were up for it."

Despite the cold, a fierce sweat starts forming on my brow. If our voices sound like gunshots, the alarm is like detonating a nuclear bomb. No chance the Remnants sleep through it. I check the high-rise. Lights flicker on across every story of the building. We've woken the demon.

"I didn't want you to have everything on your shoulders," Evelyn says. She rubs my wrist, but I tear it away and begin to work on the ignition. It's a push button starter, which requires the key. "For once, I wanted to let you rest."

"I can't do this."

"You have to," Evelyn says. "You can."

"I need the key, Ev."

"This truck is ancient," she says. "That's why we chose it."

Remnants are already beginning to filter through the building's broken entrance, snow crunching beneath their boots. We have maybe thirty seconds to make it happen.

"You need to try," Carina says. A shot rings out, missing the truck.

Without another word, I take the knife from my waistband and plunge it into the underside of the steering column. Wires spill out. Voices and footsteps crash over the empty air, reminding us that we're living on borrowed time.

A rifle barks, and the front windshield cracks. My forehead bounces off the wheel when I duck.

"Shit!" I yank the wires, trying to separate the right ones. Hopefully this truck is as ancient as Evelyn thinks. Otherwise we're all dead. More bullets pepper the truck's chassis. Then Jana's amplified voice sends my blood cold.

"If you steal from us, you will be executed without trial." I try to tune it out, but her words boom across the plains. "You cannot be allowed to leave."

A blue spark bursts from the wires, blackening my fingertips. I lick the wound, and get back in for another try.

"Twenty yards, Luke," Evelyn says. "They're running—

The engine roars to life just as a thunderous *boom* rocks the truck. The passenger side window vaporizes into a shower of glass. A spatter of blood splashes across the worn leather interior. With all the adrenaline pumping through my veins, I can't be sure it's not me.

I throw the truck into reverse and jam the accelerator to the floor. Too late, I actually check what's behind me—a massive eighteen wheeler, ten tons of immovable metal. I slam on the brake, softening the impact. We still scream into the front fender in a torrid crash of metal.

There's no time to inspect the damage. Almost breaking the shifter off, I throw the truck into drive. We separate from the other vehicle with a metal-on-metal shriek, and then we're roaring forward.

A Remnant sits directly in front of us, steadying his rifle against his bike's handlebars. I mash the accelerator, and the bike crunches underneath the truck's wheels. He flies over, his bones shattering as he bounces off the windshield and tumbles back into the ruined soil.

Shots pepper the truck as I peel out, running parallel to the way station's gates.

Jana screams orders at her loyal subjects. "You cannot let him leave. He cannot leave."

Remnants frantically kickstart their bikes to give chase. I lean forward and shake the rifle off my back.

She's more concerned about the open sign of defiance than anything I can offer. She wasn't ever really on board with the western push. The only reason we even found this "paradise" was because I forced her hand. Now that she has the power, she's just a less vicious version of her father.

"Can you shoot 'em if they get close?"

There's no answer, and I remember the blood. Icy dread gripping my chest, I turn my head slowly to look in the passenger seat. Evelyn cradles Carina, trying to stop the bleeding. An open wound spits and sputters around Carina's chest.

"How bad is it?"

Still no answer.

I check the mirrors. The bikes are finally running at a decent clip, but they're a good quarter mile behind. Still, on the endless open plains, they can give chase for however long it takes. The truck's tires kick up chunks of frozen soil, making it hard to get a good read on how many are behind us. I check on Evelyn, who clutches Carina tighter.

"Tell me what you need," I say.

"The supplies in the back."

I check our pursuers and try to assess the situation. How many bikes can Jana afford for vengeance? A half dozen? Each one is precious, and get too far out, without refueling...

It's a gamble, but glancing at Carina's ashen face, we're out of options. After another three miles, I pull the truck into a screeching stop.

"Put both doors out," I say, getting down from the cab. "And stay low."

Evelyn hurries out to search the truck bed for medical supplies. From the back tailgate, I aim and fire, blowing one of the pursuers straight off his bike. The errant vehicle acts like a missile, taking out two of his companions as the other bikes swerve around the wreckage. Our pursuers slow down when they realize the game has changed.

The riders dismount, using their vehicles for cover. With everything stationary, I finally manage a good count: three more.

A gunshot cracks over my head and rips through the door's window. Realizing I'm completely exposed, I hurry toward the front of the truck. My breath is heavy, freezing almost on contact with the atmosphere. In the distance, I hear more bikes.

Reinforcements.

A hail of gunfire rings out across the plains.

I realize they're shooting at Evelyn. She hasn't returned with her medical supplies.

"Fuck." I spring around the open driver's-side door. I squeeze off shot after shot, *chunk-chunk-chunk*, spent shell casings spitting past my frozen cheeks. The Rems stays behind their bikes as I continue the salvo.

Evelyn pops out from beneath the canvas and slides over the edge of the truck bed. Not a moment too soon, because my clip goes empty, the hollow *click* easily audible across the still plains. I dive beneath the truck as they return fire. Red glass showers into the snow as they spray us with bullets.

I roll over, and for the first time I'm reminded how sick I was a few days before. Stifling a cough, I stare at the broken taillight and wait for everything to stop. The red glass reminds me of the blood inside the cab.

I check my pockets and find that I'm out of bullets. All the same, when there's a brief break in the gunfire, I click the clip back into place, giving the impression that I'm ready for another firefight. With a deep breath, I roll out from beneath the truck and pop up, rifle scope at eye-level, like I'm about to unleash hellfire on them.

Then, I instead turn and sprint the five feet to the

cab, hopping in just as they realize my bluff. Angry shouts and curses flood across the plains. I don't even shut the door—the engine is idling, and I just floor it.

They make the wrong move and try to take us out. Bullets chase our battered vehicle, but I'm swerving like a drunk, and we're quickly too far away to hit. The sounds of our pursuers are swallowed by the growl of the engine and the harsh whistle of the wind. Reaching out to grab the flapping door, I breathe a minor sigh of relief. With the broken window, though, the cab doesn't get much warmer.

I listen carefully, trying to discern whether two people are breathing. Finally, unable to tell, I venture a look at the passenger side.

Carina's eyes are closed.

"She sleeping?"

Evelyn just shakes her head.

And the ice in my stomach turns into something much chillier.

19 | FROZEN WASTES

THE ONLY WORDS Evelyn and I share for the next thousand miles involve where we should head next. We both agree that the Lost Plains are still the Remnants' domain, despite the march of the NAS. If we stay, they have a good chance of tracking us down. Now seems like a good time to go where no one can find us.

Heading directly toward the Gray Desert is one option. But with Blackstone's search party already coming through the wreckage—and maybe a new faction lying in wait—we can't just waltz across the border. And after what happened, we need time to regroup and plan our next move.

So me and Evelyn agree on the destination. Then I drive straight through. We only stop when the fuel light comes on. Evelyn's plan wasn't perfect, but she did the best she could under the circumstances. Still, the guilt is clearly etched into her face. It might never go away.

Periodically, I'll look over at Carina's pale face. She looks peaceful, like she's just taking a nap. Her silver chain rattles with a gentle *clink* every time we hit a pothole or tree branch—which is pretty often. The sound makes a lump form in my throat.

Eventually, we coax the bullet-riddled truck to a dilapidated border station with rows of tollbooths. A sign announces that we should have our passports ready. But as we pass through the ruined gates, no one tries to stop us. Supposedly the only place in the world with any human survivors is the North American Circle—excuse me, the New Allied States.

Which makes the Frozen Wastes as good a place to hide out as any. The place has earned its name. The weather around the way station high-rise resembled a tropical retreat in comparison to the permafrost chill that passes for weather here. The truck's temperature sensor stopped working fifty miles ago, but last I checked, it was thirty below. Translucent white ice coats everything.

Once we're clear of the tollbooths, I pull off a few miles ahead, at an abandoned rest stop. Rows and rows of battery pods—to charge electric cars—sit dormant, ready to service vehicles that will never come again.

"I need to patch this window," I say, teeth chattering as I open the door. I almost slip when I step down from the cab. Evelyn follows me toward the cargo bed, lifting up the canvas so that I can search through our supplies.

"She was a nice girl," I say. "Carina."

"That's all you can say?"

"She wasn't a church mouse between the sheets."

Evelyn laughs, although it's tinged with sadness. "You always know what to say, don't you?"

"Life's a bitch."

"Nice philosophy."

"It's not all bad," I say, rummaging through a toolbox. Finding nothing, I slam it against the side. "It's not your fault."

Her gloved hands squeeze my shoulders. "We'll have to let it go."

"I don't even want to kill Jana," I say, emerging from beneath the canvas. I've found nothing that will help patch the windows. "I should, but—everyone's just trying to survive. In their own way."

I glance back at the cab, where Carina's brown hair, slightly matted with blood, presses against the rear windshield.

"We're almost out of fuel," Evelyn says, her voice choked up. "We won't reach the Gray Desert with what we have."

"Add it to the list of supplies," I say. "Some big guns would be nice, too."

I rub my face and look at the rest stop. It's covered in graffiti—French, from what I can tell—and doesn't look particularly inviting. Ramses walks along the frozen concrete, urging me to follow him inside.

"At least she won't have to see these visions," I say. "I don't know how much longer I got, Ev."

"It'll be all right."

But neither of us really believes that. Eventually, we settle on cutting up the canvas. Evelyn lines it with Carina's parka before we set out on the road again.

I find myself worrying that she'll be cold.

It's gonna be hard to let things go.

*

TWO CONSECUTIVE NIGHTS of driving straight through is an unpleasant proposition. With a wordless conversation, Evelyn and I decide to set up camp in an abandoned country house. I pull the truck around back, hiding it behind the skeletal remains of the ruined garage.

After I check to make sure the house is empty, we unload the few things we'll need for the night.

On our last trip, Evelyn stops before we reach the stairs.

"We have to bury her."

I wipe my nose and let out a long sigh. It's a few moments before I can form words. "I don't know if I can do that."

"She loved you, Luke."

"That's not what I meant." I can't face her. But from the words, I realize that, over the past month, Carina and Evelyn got close. True friendship, despite their differences. "I wasn't thinking."

"I'll start a fire," Evelyn says. "There's a wood stove inside."

"Keep it small."

She nods, then walks up the stairs without another word. I head toward the cargo bed and grab a shovel. After trekking into the middle of a ruined field that once bore crops, I slam the shovel against the hard ground.

I might as well be trying to dig a hole through concrete. Two minutes later, the tip of the shovel is bent beyond repair. Unleashing a disgusted stream of expletives, I fling it across the barren landscape.

Despair might not be helpful in a moment like this, but it's hard to have hope. My last ally has turned against me, killed one of the only friends I had left in this word. A bitter grin creases my cracked lips.

Was Carina a friend?

Is Evelyn my friend?

Perhaps a construct like friendship is antiquated. The modern world is like mercury—it slithers away the moment you think you have it corralled. Alliances between entire factions change with quicksilver ease. What that says about the bonds between individuals, I don't know.

The pale moon claws through the cloudy sky, casting forlorn slivers of light across the field. As I stare into nothingness, the smell of wood smoke from the house gives me an idea. I return to the truck and rummage through our remaining supplies. This might be a waste of things we'll need later, but maybe holding on to a piece of your humanity is more important.

Or we could've been fooling ourselves all along— maybe we were always savages.

My fingers locate a box of shotgun shells buried in one of the food satchels. These will do.

I return to the middle of the field, shells, a rope soaked in diesel fuel and a book of matches clutched in my hands. Using the ruined shovel, I managed to etch out a divot in the frozen ground. It's no more than a quarter foot deep, but it feels like a major accomplishment.

In this hole, I pile the shells over the end of the fuel covered rope. Then I unfurl the rope until I'm a safe distance away. After a few false starts with the matches, I manage to get one lit. I drop it onto the rope. An orange flame greedily sprints across the fuel-soaked fibers. It's not long after that before a small explosion erupts.

Evelyn rushes out of the house without her jacket. She's holding a .38.

"What the hell are you doing?"

I stare at the dying orange flame. "Burying her."

It takes a moment for her to put everything together. Then she simply says, "Dinner's waiting when you're done."

The soil isn't forgiving, but the explosion has widened a hole and warmed the ground just enough for me to actually dig. It's a shallow grave, but it's the best I can do. Deeper down, the cold earth simply won't give at all.

When I pat the last bit of frozen soil down, I kneel and close my eyes.

"I'm sorry," I say, rubbing Carina's metal chain between my fingers.

Then I rise up and walk inside, where I find Evelyn hard at work, hacking apart a chair.

"Needed it for the fireplace," she says. "And then I figured…"

I walk around the table, so that her work isn't clouded in shadow.

It's a cross, small and slightly asymmetrical.

"Neither of us care, but she thought God was looking out for her." Evelyn shrugs. "Guess she was wrong, but still."

"She would've liked that."

Before the ground freezes again, I walk back out and push the cross into the soil.

I don't believe it, but I say, "Maybe death is a better fate."

Then I head back to the house and shut the door.

Because, for some reason, I still want to figure out how to stay alive.

20 | BORDERS

It's FUNNY HOW quickly the human body adjusts. When morning comes, my thick clothes are stuck to my skin from sweat. The stove's glowing embers are almost dead, but I still want to strip everything off. It can't be more than zero degrees.

Evelyn is still asleep, huddled in one of the few chairs we didn't sacrifice to the fire.

Careful not to wake her, I sneak past into the house's foyer. The stairs leading to the second floor have rotted away from decades of abandonment. Whatever secrets remain up there, I won't ever find them.

I look past the stairwell, toward the kitchen. Dawn light filters in through the streaked windows. Before the kitchen, there's a door leading to a cellar. We briefly entertained the idea of exploring it last night, but going too far from the fire was a non-starter for us both.

I push the door open, the hinges creaking. White paint flicks off and crumbles when I touch the surface. I take the steep stairs one at a time, cautiously putting about half my weight on each to test the structural integrity. They groan and protest, but I manage to make it down with breaking an ankle.

Thin slivers of light cut through a dirty window in the corner. The floor is unfinished concrete, stained by dirt. A washing machine and dryer sit idly, rust gnawing at their edges. Nothing moves, and I get the impression that I'm the first living creature to set foot down here in years.

Methodically, I work my way around the basement. The pantry shelves are bare, nothing but empty bottles and barren sacks of grain. Behind the washer I find a rusted shotgun. It's probably no good, but I take it anyway.

A scream cuts through the morning tranquility. Clutching the flaking metal firearm tight in my hands, I pound up the stairs—caution be damned—and race toward the living room.

"You bitch. Nice girls don't bite."

"I'm not a nice girl."

A dirty, feral looking man has his hands gripped around Evelyn's throat. She's kicking and gasping, but he's got a wiry sort of quickness that allows him to get out of the way.

He looks at me, and the shotgun, and then lets go.

"All right, all right," he says. "Don't shoot me in my own home."

"This isn't your home," I say. I don't raise the shotgun. He must know it's useless from its appearance. But I think he's decided that two of us is too much to handle.

At least for now.

A patchy beard graces his face. With the wisps of hair and sheer volume of dirt caking his skin, it's impossible to tell what he actually looks like. White eyes stare out at me, as if from behind holes in a curtain.

He gives an easy laugh. "All right, all right. Martin saw the house and wanted to take a little look."

His clothes are threadbare—holey jeans, boots with the soles coming off. A jacket that's not fit for a chilly fall day, let alone the temperatures here.

"You with Blackstone?" I step forward, brandishing the shotgun like a club. It might not fire any bullets, but it's still a heavy chunk of metal.

"Who the hell's Blackstone? Man, Martin don't know any Blackstone." His eyes are nervous, now. I'm more of a wildcard than he predicted. Evelyn rubs her throat and spits out a little blood.

"You okay?" I say.

"Better before this smelly bastard was around," Evelyn says.

"No need for name calling, bitch," the man says.

I catch him in the jaw with the shotgun stock, and he crumbles to one knee. "If you're with Blackstone, or Slick, or Daniels, or any of them—"

"I don't know anything, man," he says. "Fucking hell, I saw smoke, came in to see if I could steal some food. Your girl came outta the corner and tried to hit Martin with a damn chair leg."

I glance over, beneath the table. There's a splintered piece of lumber sitting at an odd angle. Evelyn shrugs, still massaging her neck.

"Why didn't you call me up," I say.

"Thought I could handle one piece of shit," she says.

"Again, with the names, bitch." I raise up to hit him with the shotgun again, but he waves his hands. "All right, all right. I'll change my ways. Martin knows how to survive."

"Who's Martin?" I say. "Where's Martin?" The thought of two crack-heads scurrying around does not have me excited.

"Me," he says, getting to his feet somewhat unsteadily. "Martin von Amsterdam VI. Got a little king's blood on my momma's side, way back."

Martin's lying, but he gets points for spinning an amusing yarn. "Okay, Martin. Why don't you tell me why I shouldn't leave you tied up for the wolves?"

Panic bursts across his face. "I, uh, I—well, you can't kill Martin." His yellow teeth flash an uneasy smile. "Martin can be pretty helpful, if you know what you're looking for."

I walk slowly across the room to help Evelyn up. Low, so Martin can't hear, I say, "Get packed."

"What are you gonna do with him?"

"Just get packed," I say, keeping my eyes on Martin. He's watching us with intense curiosity. Can't blame him. His life depends on whatever I decide.

"You know who he is, right?" Evelyn says, her lips close to my ear.

I give Martin an unfriendly smile, then shake my head. "She's not pleased about your entrance."

"She tried to kill Martin, though," he says, wringing his hands together. Blackened swirls are visible around his cuticles. Tough to tell whether it's just grime, or indicative of a larger problem. He's got the waifish constitution of someone who hasn't been eating much.

"He used to be in that pop-rock band," Evelyn says, low. "Ran off the road, high on coke. Killed the lead singer of his band in the crash. They deported him, when the Frozen Wastes were still Canada."

Martin's sunken, unblinking eyes yearn to hear our conversation. He's so fucked up that the poor bastard probably thinks he can do it through sheer force of will.

"Any good," I say, in a low voice.

"What?"

"His band?"

"The Rhinoceros Pioneers," Evelyn says. "They had that song, 'Need You, Love You, Can't Have You,' which was decent."

I nod—not that this trivia changes the current situation. I wink at Evelyn, indicating that she should get packing.

Then I say, "You need to apologize to my friend."

"Martin is so sorry," he says, dropping to his knees, his voice taking on a pathetic whine. "I'm so sorry." He crawls on the floor toward me boots and places his head on the leather, rubbing it like a loyal pet. "Please don't kill me."

He looks up at me with the most pathetic hang-dog look. The pupils are pinned as hell, which is when I realize that Martin has no idea that this gun doesn't work. He's barely here. Shame he got deported before HIVE was a thing. This guy is living the analog HIVE existence. That has way more side effects, judging from his appearance.

Somewhere, Ramses barks. I ignore the hallucination, gripping the rusted shotgun tight.

"You said you can be helpful."

"I can't be helpful," Martin says. "But Martin can be helpful."

I don't have time for his rock-god alternate ego thing.

"If Martin doesn't cut the bullshit, he's gonna be left for the wolves, okay?" Evelyn slips past through the hallway door. A frigid burst of wind streams into the room, making me shiver. Martin barely seems to notice, but then, he's already shaking like a leaf in a storm.

"Yeah, um, sorry man," he says, with this *far out* kind of vibe, "it's just that, if I think about it too much, my head hurts, you know?"

"Think about what?"

"My life," Martin says with a sad look. Then he pukes on my boots. I kick him in the ribs and shake off my feet.

"Aw shit, come on."

"Martin's sorry," he says between groans. He holds his stomach. "Morphine, man, just a little taste."

"You don't get shit." I'm not going down this road again. One assisted suicide is enough for one month. I step over his body and head toward the door.

"Wait," Martin says. "I know this place."

"A junkie rock musician *and* an outdoorsman," I say, pausing in the doorway. I stare at an askew portrait of the owner of this house. She has a severe look, no make-up, a constipated expression across her lips. Definitely wouldn't approve of her current boarders. "You're a regular fucking renaissance man."

"Hey, just cause your piece of ass tried to beat Martin's ass and he defended himself—"

I wheel around. He sloshes into his vomit, moving at what, for him, must be the speed of light.

"You're lucky I don't kill you," I say. "You know that?"

He breaks down into sobs. "You can't leave me. That's the same thing."

"You made it here. You'll make it out."

"Man, Martin's been wandering for days," he says between sniffles. "I did my last bump when I saw this place. This is the end of the road."

"Better use those outdoor skills."

"They'll get me," Martin says. "Don't leave."

I stare at this wasted wreck of a man, remembering

Sid's cryptic words about another faction. Then again, if these are the only two sources I have, that doesn't exactly constitute irrefutable evidence.

"I might have a couple meds in the truck," I say. "Maybe."

"I tried to steal it," Martin says. "I won't lie. But I can't hotwire shit."

"Let's focus on who's trying to get you."

"They don't care about Martin," he says, shaking his head. "It's about the world, man."

"*Who.*" As much as I want to continue this conversation well into the afternoon, we need to get on the road. If the soldier Jana tortured was telling the truth, a scout party is already looking for the Gifted Minds Research Institute. When they find it, it's much game over.

"They're settin' up in the South," Martin says. "All over the world."

"Forget it," I say. He's clearly talking gibberish. The rest of the world was wiped out in the floods over twenty years ago. No one's heard anything from the other continents since the North American Circle formed in 2026. Hard to communicate when you're drowning in the rising tides.

I walk over and kneel beneath the table. Pick up the busted piece of furniture. Martin cowers like an abused dog, but I just walk past and toss it in the stove. The dying embers hiss and spark, before greedily beginning to devour the new fuel.

"Have fun by yourself," I say. "We see you again, we'll shoot you on sight."

"The Oceanic Coalition," he whispers. "They're coming for everyone. They're already in the Gray Desert."

I pause before I shut the door to the wood stove. "How do you know about the Gray Desert?"

"Martin knows about lots of things," he says, scrambling to his feet. "He can be useful." I wince as he stumbles closer, the pungent aroma of puke, piss and rancid sweat mixing with the scent of wood smoke.

"Just, uh, just wait over there."

"But Martin can tell you—"

"Martin can tell me from where he's standing," I say, covering my mouth to stifle a gag. The front porch creaks, but I don't take my eyes off the decrepit rock star. Evelyn enters the room.

"We're all ready to go."

"Martin told me something interesting about the rest of the world," I say. "Maybe Sid wasn't lying about another faction."

"He's been doing hard drugs since he was fifteen, Luke," Evelyn says. "His brain is toast."

"Martin takes objection to that diagnosis," he says. Then, with a smile, channeling some long-lost charisma, "But you can play nurse with me any time."

"I'll pass."

"You know I wrote that song," Martin says. "I could see it in your eyes." He does this weak kind of rock 'n roll pelvic thrust that, once upon a time, probably worked real good. Here, in a frozen and abandoned house at the fringes of a ruined world, it's about as useful as a dog capable of standing on its hind legs.

"Focus, man," I say, snapping my fingers. His eyes trace back over the room slowly, finally settling on me. "The Oceanic Coalition."

"They've got a coupla outposts up here," Martin says. "They're planning an assault from all sides."

"How do you know this?"

"Most people like Martin a lot more," he says. "They talk to him. Give him food."

"Somehow I doubt that," I say.

"We need to move out," Evelyn says, tapping an invisible watch on her wrist. "Over a thousand miles to go."

Martin practically leaps at me before I'm able to react. Tugging at me coat, he says, "You'll need Martin to make it across the Frozen Wastes."

"I don't think anyone's needed Martin for a long time, now."

"I can trade," Martin says. "I know things about the Oshies."

"Clever name."

"Martin can't take credit for it."

"How magnanimous of him." I shoot Evelyn a look. This guy's craziness could be viral. I'm starting to think I'm talking to two different men, instead of one schizophrenic disaster.

The fire pops and crackles. There's a long silence, then Martin says, in a surprisingly even and sane tone, "I can help you survive. I looked in your truck and you don't have enough fuel to make it a thousand miles."

I raise an eyebrow at Evelyn. "Your call."

"He's right," she says, and then brings her hand to her throat. "On the other hand…"

I grimace and sigh. This is what it's come to. If the Remnants were the lowest rung of ally, Martin, king of his own imaginary paradise, has to be in the basement below the ladder.

"Trial run, man," I say. He looks about ready to hug me. "One condition, though."

"Anything, Martin will do anything."

I bet he will.

And that's what I'm afraid of.

21 | BARTER

AFTER WE HEAT up some water and clean Martin up—like hell we're going to give him new clothes smelling like this—we get on the road. He's not pleased about the conditional nature of traveling with us, something he makes us well aware of by banging on the truck bed.

"He might freeze," Evelyn says.

"We gave him enough blankets. He keeps his head down and wrapped tight, he'll be all right."

"There." Evelyn points at a ring of smoke in the distance. I slow down, the truck's tires slipping a little bit on the icy highway. I weave around an abandoned car and peer through the cracked windshield.

"We got a backup plan, this thing goes south?"

"I don't think so."

"Great," I say. "This time, you'll die and I'll be all alone with this fuck."

She shoots me a withering glance, but says nothing. I realize I stepped in it, a little too late.

"I wasn't saying it was your fault—"

"But you kinda just did."

"I'm just tired. You know what I meant."

"I do," Evelyn says, and closes her eyes. With all the

cracks and breaks in the windows, wind streams in past our canvas patches. Her blonde hair flows about her face, shielding it from view. I open my mouth, then decide to let the matter alone.

Up ahead, the highway narrows into a single lane. That's because whoever's established this fine settlement has organized the cars in such a way that I'm forced into the left lane. The arrangement makes me nervous, so I stop before the point of no return.

I leave the truck idling and step out. I grab the rifle for show, even though I have no bullets. I walk around to the bed and rap my fingers on the tailgate.

"Martin." There's no answer in the frozen silence. Maybe I did kill him. "*Martin.*"

"I was having the nicest dream, man," Martin says. "It was from our London show, the last one we did in 2024. These two chicks, man, one of them was eating my—"

I punch the truck, denting the metal. It has the intended effect. Gets him to shut up.

"Come out for a second."

"Can Martin ride in the front?"

"No, Martin can't ride in the front until he proves himself," I say. "Remember?"

He whines sullenly, unbefitting of a man over forty. "All these rules." But he emerges from the canvas, his stringy hair plastered to his pale lips. Hard to determine whether he looks worse than when I last saw him.

Cold therapy does wonders for some people. Or so I've heard.

He peeks out over the front of the truck, holding his arms out like he's teetering on a balance beam.

"This is it," Martin says, nodding with intense vigor. "They've traded with Martin before."

"What'd they give him—you?" I roll my eyes slightly and remind myself not to get sucked in to the craziness. Luckily, my own hallucinations don't feel the need to chime in. The sooner I'm rid of Ramses, the better. Solve your own issues before helping others, right? Or just solve your own issues because they're the only ones you really give a crap about.

Martin makes a sniffling sound, too deliberate to be from the cold. "They have all sorts of things. They're really good scavengers, man."

"And are the Oshies *nasty* scavengers?"

"Everyone's nasty when they need to be."

It's the cogent thoughts that throw me. Life is mostly about expectations. When you're bracing for crazy, lucid insights gut punch you. Probably would have the same reaction if I stumbled upon an orphanage out here. The contrast might fry my brain.

"So we're doing this," I say. "I'm driving through."

"Yes."

"You're gonna die if you're screwing us. I'll kill you before they can get you."

He turns and smiles, his yellow teeth and sunken eyes making him look like an exhumed demon. But it's not scary. More just emblematic of the times.

"Martin loves drugs," he says. "He doesn't screw around about drugs."

Some things are best left unanswered. I climb back into the cab and put the truck in drive.

And then we enter the gauntlet.

*

FROM THE SMOKE, I was expecting a densely populated town like the Gunpowder Hills. What I find is a cluster of ten cabins, a general store and a bar. No one comes out to greet us. I pull right into the middle of the buildings—what one could consider center square—and cut the engine. The fuel light blinks. We're running down to our last few gallons of diesel.

Smoke puffs out of the general store's chimneys. The other buildings are dormant.

Too late to make a fast escape, now. They've probably been watching us for the past fifty miles. Or it's possible they haven't—no one expects visitors this far up north. A wicked wind chill reminds me why when I step down from the truck. I leave the empty rifle on the seat.

Evelyn murmurs, having fallen asleep somewhere along the fifteen miles of single-lane cars. With the endless white expanses stretching out around the tiny frozen settlement as far as I can see, I'm beginning to think that the one-lane highway was created to pass the time, rather than for any practical reasons.

No eyes lurk behind the curtainless windows. No one greets us.

"Hello?" I call. "I'm here to trade."

A wolf howls in the distance. Not quite the response I was looking for. I step toward the general store, which has the word "store" painted on it in a number of different languages.

A foot of powder up against the wood indicates that no one's been in or out since the last snowfall. I knock anyway, lest I be mistaken for a thief. The laws of the Frozen Wastes are pretty easy to imagine: most people will be shot on sight. You have to give others a compelling reason to let you live.

The dull thud is swallowed by the whistling wind. Light footsteps crumple in the snow behind me.

"Not much trading going on," I say.

"Martin was last here a year ago."

"It would've been nice for Martin to tell me that before I spent the last of our fuel."

He points toward the window. "Maybe we don't have to trade at all." Before I can say anything, he drags a fistful of ice off the ground and hurls it at the glass. The pane shatters with a splintering crack.

Immediately, my heart rate rises. "Why the hell did you do that?" I imagine that we've just failed an invisible test—whether we, as outsiders, are trustworthy. But none of the cabin doors open. No one comes rushing out. I begin to breathe easier. Martin walks over to me. Even in the sub-zero cold, I can still smell the faintest trace of sick on him. "Here." He holds out a hand.

"What is it?"

"I found it near one of the other cabins." He walks over to the window and begins scraping away the jagged slivers in the frame. "Don't worry."

I stare down at what he handed me.

It's a human finger.

22 | OPERATIONS

THE OSHIE'S OUTPOST is abandoned, frozen in time. The smoke from the general store was merely the exhaust from a still-functioning heating system. Dried blood and overturned mugs paint a picture of struggle. But most of the cabins, once we smash our way in, remain untouched. I stare at the hardened bowl of oatmeal sitting on the hand-carved wooden table.

Whoever came through and killed them, though, was kind enough to leave the cupboards well-stocked. As much as I don't want to admit it, sparing Martin was the right move.

The general store holds the greatest bounties, so I let Evelyn handle it. She's got her .38 ready, in case Martin pulls any bullshit. But his mind is too far gone to make any elaborate plans. After raiding the pharmaceuticals cabinet, he's spent the last few hours in a babbling stupor. I'm thankful she gets to babysit him, instead of me.

There's a journal next to the oatmeal, which I thumb through. The writer doesn't say much about the Frozen Wastes, or the Oshies—other than that living on land, after years of surviving at sea and on ocean platforms, is like heaven.

Folks have really low standards. Although going from the turbulent ocean to a permafrost encrusted wasteland is like venturing from a bar filled with dudes to one with that one girl who, if you squint hard enough at the end of the night, is passable. Survival has always been about lying to yourself—pretending that not good enough is more than enough.

I close the journal when it starts rambling off into what happened. The writing is fast and hurried. Quite frankly, whatever happened here only matters to those who lived and died through it. Like our own little skirmish on the edge of the Lost Plains, a hundred years from now, it never really will have happened at all. How long until Carina's lonely cross is covered in frost?

Maybe it's already buried.

I stand up from the table and give a final scan of the room. I've already taken all the food stuffs, anything that might be worth trading. In the far corner is a small wooden cabinet, its crooked doors designed by an imperfect maker. When I look inside, it's the jackpot.

An operational map of the Oshies' plans.

I trace my finger along the borders, examining the series of outposts they've already established in the Gray Desert. The map has no scale, but one of the dots is just south of Seattle. Despite not knowing what these ocean-faring people stand for, hope rises in my chest.

Surely they won't have given into the New Allied States' scouts without a battle. True, that means when I finally set foot in the Gray Desert, I'll be entering a war zone. But that conflict might buy us the necessary time to reach the Gifted Minds Research Institute.

A violent tremor causes me to drop the map. I slump to the floor as my synapses go haywire. My foot seizes uncontrollably, banging against the wood floor in a hap-hazard rhythm. My fingernails dig into my palms, ripping through the cold-cracked flesh. Head knocking against the cabin's walls, vision shuttering off and on, I just try to hang on. It's like I'm an observer—my body failing me, mind fraying in all directions—helpless to stop it.

Five minutes later, covered in a cold sweat, the episode abates. The map is a crumpled mess, from where I've rolled on it. I drag myself over and try to smooth it out with trembling fingers. Fortunately, it has not been ruined.

Evelyn appears at the cabin's broken window and knocks. "Find something?"

"Our salvation."

"Not you, too," Evelyn says. "The last hour, I've been hearing from Martin about how one time he saw Jesus in the bathroom of a dive bar in Soho." She presses her nose against the frosted pane to take a closer look. "It's getting worse, isn't it?"

"Just a little cold, is all." I try to plant my palm against the hard floor, show that I'm all right. But my elbow buckles under the weight. "I'll be okay."

"Let me help," she says, starting to open the window. Lilacs sweep through the small, cozy room. The wood stove crackles merrily. Another time, another era, this could be a place to forget all our troubles. But in this life it's just a checkpoint, we'll have to roll through.

"Just…keep going with the store."

"You look like you're about to die." She's hanging halfway inside, waist over the window sill. A breeze rustles her blonde hair.

"I got it, Ev." The strength in my voice startles me. Ramses even barks in solidarity. "Just finish up."

"All right." She drops back into the snow with a light crunch, gives me a final look of concern, then heads back to the general store.

I drag my hands across the rough floorboards and open up the map again. This outpost was one of only two in the Frozen Wastes. The other is closer to the Atlantic Ocean. Not the direction I'm trying to head.

The rest of the vast territory is simple blank.

I swallow hard, but then I smile.

The way people have been acting lately, emptiness can't be a bad thing.

23 | THE GRAY DESERT

THE LONG DRIVE across the Frozen Wastes is the best kind of boring. No surprises, no setbacks and no more unpredictable strangers. Whenever we see signs of a settlement, we immediately make a detour. Strangers are a wild card more dangerous than any faction. At least we know what Blackstone and the others stand for. Out here, you could stumble upon things far worse.

Martin grumbles frequently about our anti-social behavior once he runs through his stock of prescription meds. But he gets to ride in the cab, now, so he can't complain all that much.

It's the middle of February when we reach the border of the Gray Desert. Fortunately, the Oshies' outpost was stocked for years of independent survival. There were so many supplies that we couldn't fit all of them in the poor truck.

Evelyn rides the brakes as we approach the broken gates. They're little more than a pile of jumbled rubble. The 9.3 quake must've reached this far north. She's been doing most of the driving, since my hallucinations have gotten worse and Martin is obviously a non-starter due to his dubious driving history. Ramses is now a constant companion, a hundred pounds of imaginary dog that whines incessantly in my ear.

For her part, Evelyn seems to have escaped the brunt of the damage. Occasionally she'll get an odd look in her eye, and I'll know that she's having a little flashback. But, for whatever reason, the residual effects haven't hit her nearly as hard. It'd be nice if Carina was still around, have someone to commiserate with. But she's gone. I haven't forgotten about Kid Vegas, though. It might be ten years from now, but he'll be lying in his own unmarked grave before I die.

We've heard nothing about the New Allied States. The sky is clear enough to get satellite reception, but there's no coverage up north. Not surprising—that'd be a waste of valuable resource.

The motor chugs as the truck stops. It's midafternoon, but a sort of ashy film covers the glowing sun. Whether it's because we're getting closer to the volcanic eruption, or simply because the day is overcast, I can't tell. A splintered sign indicates that we're about to connect with I5 as British Columbia—*The Best Place on Earth*—bids us farewell.

"Why'd you stop," I say. My head pounds. The last couple weeks have been brutal. I glance at Martin, who also looks to be in pain, although for different reasons.

"Eventually we're gonna have to walk," Evelyn says. "Want to make sure you're up for that before we head through."

The notion sound unappealing, but I say, "That won't be a problem."

"And him?"

"He'll have to make his own decisions," I say, glancing at the shaking man in the throes of withdrawal. "He's been all right."

Annoying at times, sure. Could do without the third person affectation. But we wouldn't have made it this far without him, and allies are in general short supply.

"And you swear that it's along Interstate 5?" Evelyn says.

"That's what I've seen." Putting our lives in the hands of my misfiring neurons is quite the leap of faith. But it's not like we've got great alternatives.

Evelyn gently maneuvers the truck through the wreckage. A sign welcomes us to the United States on the other side. The Circle never got around to fully putting their stamp on this place, even when it was called the Western Stronghold. Vestiges of an old civilization abound.

We travel another fifteen miles before the interstate becomes impassable. A thin layer of ash covers everything that isn't touched by the frost.

I wake Martin.

"Martin is sleeping."

"We're walking," I say, then I get out. I help Evelyn pack what we can carry—food, mainly, and the pistols and munition we found in the general store. The Oshies' operational map is tucked safely in my back pocket. All the outposts are further south, where the climate is more hospitable.

The heavy pack digs into my shoulders. I watch as Evelyn adjusts the straps on hers. We hand Martin the lightest load, and he still almost crumbles beneath the weight.

"Martin can't carry this, man," he says with a whine. His frame is slightly less gaunt, but he still can't weigh more than a hundred pounds. "I can't do it."

I rub my mouth and cough. Fine ash is carried everywhere by the omnipresent wind. Recalling Sid's vicious respiratory infection, I take a precaution, stripping apart a spare shirt. I tie the strips together around my mouth and nose to form a makeshift mask.

Evelyn and Martin do the same. It's not exactly high-tech, but it'll have to do for now.

Then we begin to walk. Two miles later, we hit a sign telling us that Seattle is 119 miles away. I run the calculations in my head. Altogether, we're over 200 miles from our destination. Martin breathes heavily on the side of the frozen interstate.

Evelyn approaches me and says, "We need to keep moving."

"We'll never make it," I say. "At fifteen miles a day, that's over eighteen days. Probably closer to a month with all the breaks we'll need to take."

I already miss the bullet-battered truck. But the road's surface looks like it's been shelled by missiles. I glance back at the forest of felled Douglas firs, toppled against each other like twigs tossed into a pile by a small child. The destruction is absolute.

And we haven't even reached civilization yet.

It's difficult to imagine what the center of the earthquake zone looks like. Even the Rems' dirt bikes would have difficult navigating this landscape.

The peeling sign also tells us that a motel is up ahead. Six miles. By the position of the half-obscured sun, I figure we have four hours of daylight remaining.

"We need to reevaluate," I say. "Get to the motel."

"If it's still standing," Evelyn says. "Look at this place."

"It's only six miles." A stiff wind whips a cloud of

dust past. Six miles might as well be a thousand. The motel seems further away than the entire stretch of the Frozen Wastes we already rode across.

"You're sure you can make it?" Evelyn says. The only part of her face visible is those endless brown eyes. They're marked with concern and a million other subtleties that I could spend a lifetime trying to sort out.

"I can make it. I got no other choice."

*

THREE MILES IN, and Martin collapses from exhaustion. Evelyn examines him and shakes her head.

"He's not about to die, but if he keeps walking, who knows what happens."

"Fucking junkie," I say, the vitriol of my words surprising me. Then again, I've been dealing with a hell of a trip myself. My head pounds, Ramses won't leave me the hell alone, and the visions increase in intensity with physical exhaustion.

Worry floats in Evelyn's eyes. She's out here alone, and there's no way she can carry us both. Not to mention defend herself against whatever still lurks in the overturned terrain ahead.

Martin groans and sinks deeper into the snowy ash.

"No, no, don't go to sleep," Evelyn says. She presses firmly against his thick jacket, but he just grins and smiles, clearly off somewhere much more pleasant. Then she pulls away the piece of fabric covering his mouth and slaps him as hard as she can.

He sits half upright, confused. "Something hit Martin."

"That was me," Evelyn says.

"Oh, you want to cash that check from earlier," Martin says. "Don't worry, baby, I knew you would wanna sleep with me."

Then he slumps back to the ground. Somewhere in the distance, a tree sags and moans before crashing to the ground. Birds flutter away from the forest, spooked by the sudden disturbance.

The ruined interstate stretches on endlessly, tumbled chunks of roadway dotting every inch of the visible horizon. My mind searches for futile ways that we could've gotten the truck through. A man rationalizes anything when he's half-frozen.

Adjusting the heavy pack on my shoulders, I stare at the distance for a beat longer. There's a tranquil, odd beauty to the empty landscape. Like how everything's gonna be, when humans no longer exist and the earth is reclaimed by simpler life forms.

"Here," I hear Evelyn say. "Come on, take a deep breath through your nose."

There's a familiar snuffling sound, and Martin's suddenly alive. "You said we were out."

"I lied," Evelyn says. "Aren't you happy I did, though?"

I raise an eyebrow at the barren landscape, the crisis momentarily averted by the very habit that will kill Martin if he maintains it. Irony.

Sometimes the wrong move is the right one.

*

WE ARRIVE AT the Pacific Lodge just as the sun ducks below the horizon. Martin's narcotics are wearing off, so Evelyn has to prop him up the last two hundred yards. We pass an ash and frost encrusted van in the otherwise empty parking lot.

The Pacific Lodge is a single story motel with a rustic, twentieth century aesthetic. There are no tracks nearby, no sign that anyone has come by in the past three years. Then again, you'd have to be crazy to come here if you weren't desperate.

"I'll check the office." I pass by a sign announcing, with pride, that they have free high-speed internet and a complimentary continental breakfast. It makes me wonder if this place was abandoned two decades before the quake even hit.

The office door hangs slightly ajar, and the filing cabinets and furniture are all overturned. Deep cracks run through the plaster, exposing the beams above. But whoever designed this little motel didn't do a bad job, considering the place is still standing. No small feat when everything else has been leveled.

"Hurry up," Evelyn calls. "It's cold out here."

I navigate through the twisted furniture in the waiting area. Pressing both hands against the cold plastic counter, I grit my teeth and vault over. Unable to stop my momentum, I crash to the floor. Luckily, I land in the one relatively clear spot in the entire office.

I brush myself off and get up slowly, looking for the

keys. There's a poster of a fisherman holding up a fish bigger than the length of my torso. A twisted fishing pole lies in the corner, snapped in half during the quake.

Finding the keys in this mess isn't likely. But it's preferable to going the nuclear route by blasting our way into the room. A closed door offers far more protection against the cold than one half-ajar. There are other considerations, too—like if the power is still working. Could be that there's a generator switch in here somewhere—

"Get the hell off me," Evelyn yells. "Luke!"

I clear the counter with ease this time and tear into the frozen parking lot with my pistol drawn. Two men stand beneath the awning, near the row of rooms. One holds Evelyn, the other Martin.

"Let them go," I say, trying to keep my voice steady. Pain surges through the back of my skull. I grip the pistol stock tighter, hoping that its mere sight will encourage the men to leave.

But they don't move.

"You ain't gonna shoot," the taller one says. He's got a cowboy hat on, a strange mask shielding his face. "Hell, you idiots ain't gonna last long running around here without nothing filterin' out the ash."

"Yeah, just a bunch of morons," his short, stocky—bordering on fat—partner says. "You're all dead men."

"Best not threaten me," I say, walking closer, each step measured. Hopefully the message is that I'm in control. But, really, I'm taking tiny steps because I'm afraid if I move too quickly, I'll pass out. It's happened a couple times over the past few weeks.

"We don't want no trouble," the taller one says. "In fact, we been lookin' for you, I think."

"I don't think so," I say.

"Yeah, I recognize you," the taller one says with a nod, his cowboy hat flapping in the breeze. "From the pitchers in his house. Wouldn't you say that's the truth, Joe?"

Joe, the short one, replies, "I bet he makes the ladies real wet, Reno."

Reno, the cool tall one says, "So what's it gonna be, pretty boy? You come along with us, or things gonna get violent? Maybe you kill one of us. Hell, maybe you get us both. That could happen, right Joe?"

"Could," Joe says. "I seen a man, out on the platform, snatched by a shark a hunnerd feet long."

"Don't listen to Joe," Reno says, "he's full of shit." He spits a blackish-brown wad into the dust. "But the point stands. We ain't 'fraid to die."

"How refreshing," I say, the pistol trembling in my hand. "Let my friends go."

"We ain't gonna listen to you just because you friends with someone famous," Reno says. He takes one hand of Martin and adjusts the brim of the cowboy hat. Makes him look cool, like he means business. "Though I loved that song. What was it called?"

He hums a couple bars of it before Martin comes in and says, "You're fucking ruining it, you prick." Most life I've seen from him in a while. Apparently the artist part of him is still alive, deep within some far, recessed cave in his soul.

"You never was much of a singer, Reno," Joe says, in his rumbling, kind of stupid sounding voice. Evelyn tries to get away, but his fat fingers have a tight hold around her wrist. He doesn't hurt her, just keeps her in place, lets her know that she's not going to be making a break for it.

"True," Reno says. He loosens up his shoulders, like

he's trying to work a kink out of his lanky frame. Then he belts out a couple more bars, off-tune. It's bad enough that I wince. "That any better?"

Martin unleashes a torrent of furious expletives about how amateurs and dilettantes ruin art. Both Reno and Joe laugh. At least they're amused.

"We wasn't sure until your girlfriend yelled your name," Reno says, finally regaining his composure. "But yeah, you're Luke Stokes."

"You want the HIVE bounty?" I say. "You can have it, you let 'em both go."

"We don't care about that shit," Reno says.

"Nah, not one bit," Joe agrees.

"What we care about," Reno says. "Is making this place a little more habitable. And you can help. I figure it's fate, you appearin' while we was doing our rounds. You think that's the case, Joe?"

"Nah, I don't believe in that shit," Joe says.

"Yeah, that's probably right," Reno says. "We got a coupla cameras along the interstate. Caught y'all walking down. And I'm thinking, *hey, I seen that bastard around before.*"

"You walk all the way out here just to greet me?" I say. "That's awful kind of you."

They both share a laugh and then Reno says, "You get the five-star welcome today."

"Why's that?"

"Because you're gonna save us, kid," Joe says, like I'm some sort of dummy.

I don't say anything, but inside, I'm thinking *I've heard that before.*

24 | OPERATIONAL CONTROL

THE HELICOPTER TOUCHES down in the middle of the broken suburban street. We've been following the skeletal outline of I5 for the past hour and a half. And it's all led here: to the western Gifted Minds compound, twenty yards from the sign I've hallucinated so many times. Outside the broken chain-link fence, I see the faded, ash smeared letters: GIFTED MINDS RESEARCH INSTITUTE, WESTERN DIVISION.

Joe stays behind with Martin in the chopper. Reno is clearly lead dog. He flew the chopper. So eager to talk in the parking lot, the ride over was surprisingly silent. All I got from him was they were part of the Oshies, and they'd been trying to figure out what was going on here for the better part of a year. And, apparently, me and Matt had become their white whales.

I'm surprised by how stoic he is, with his wispy mustache and lake blue eyes, considering he just found me. But I he's used to being buffeted by fate enough that he doesn't ride it too high or too low any more.

Once we're on the ground and walking toward the sign, Reno starts talking full-tilt again.

"So you actually seen this HIVE thing up close," he says.

"You could say that." I play coy while I feel him out. No telling what the Oshies' agenda is. But their threats have been about the nicest I've encountered in this bleak new world. So I guess they score points for that. Or maybe they just remain neutral on the scorecard.

I hear gunfire in the distance. Reno sees my expression change, and he nods.

"The locals ain't too pleased about us bein' here," Reno says. "Funny thing is, I'mma local."

"Where from?"

"Tempe," Reno says. "Close enough, right?"

"Guess so," I say. "You mean the—"

"That goddamn alliance is what I mean." The skirmish stops and Reno adjusts his hat again. "Them—what do you call 'em?"

"New Allied States," I say. "I think."

"Yeah, them bastards, they've been coming at us for the past month. First the scouts, then reinforcements last week."

"How many people you got?"

"Less than them," Reno says. We pass the sign. I slow down for a beat. It's slightly surreal to see it in person, and for a moment I wonder if I'm having another flashback. But when I touch the weather-worn letters, my fingertips tell me that it's actually real.

We pass through the chain-link fence. I never set foot inside the Gifted Minds facility in New Manhattan—at least not voluntarily—but this one looks less impressive. Half of it has simply sagged into a heap of rubble, and the other part of it looks ready to crumble at any moment.

Even when it was fully upright, it definitely lacked the opulence of its more refined Eastern counterpart. It resembles a small, one-story elementary school with its drab yellow brick and bent flag pole out front.

A man hurries up to Reno's side and stands at attention.

"A message from the front, sir," the young man says. His body quakes from nervousness. He can't be more than twenty, although his face has been prematurely weathered by a harsh life spent exposed to the elements.

"Thanks," Reno says, and tips his cowboy hat. He skims the paper.

"Yes sir. It's an honor, sir." Then the kid rushes off, running like he's walking on air.

"You expect me to start calling you sir, we're gonna have a problem," I say.

"Part of bein' the leader," Reno says. "Occupational hazard."

I don't have a smart response, but Evelyn covers for me with faux reverence. "Oh my *God*. We've, like, never met anyone as powerful as a—who are you? A duke? Maybe he's even a *king*, Luke. Can you imagine that? A *king*."

She squeals with delight at the end, which forces me to stifle a laugh.

Reno tips his hat and smiles. "It's a little silly, you ask me. If people could make decisions for themselves, we wouldn't be in this mess."

"Don't tell me. Joe's your VP," I say.

This time it's Reno who laughs. It's as off-tone as his singing, but pleasantly real and easy in a way that's out of place in the world. He stops in front of the bent flag pole and says, "Nah, Joe's just an old friend."

"Those are hard to find," I say. Inside, I can see that the facility is far busier than I expected. Through the glass I watch dozens of people mill about, doing apparently important things.

"Don't have to tell me twice."

"What'd your little errand boy tell you?"

Reno arches an eyebrow, like it's too early to trust me. Then he says, "Hell, we're already deep in this." He spits on the ground. I can tell from the scent that it's mint flavored chewing tobacco. "You heard of this Kid Vegas fella?"

My jaw locks slightly when I hear that name again. But I say, "The worst kind of snake."

"That's what your brother said." Reno reaches into his pocket and takes out a big lump of chew. "At least in his papers. Hated that summabitch." He tucks the thick ball into his cheek and looks real intently inside. "The worst kind of snake. What's that?"

I don't hesitate when I answer.

"The kind you can't even tell is a snake before it's too late."

25 | RECALIBRATED

FOR A GROUP of vagrant seafarers who survived the open waters for decades, the Oceanic Coalition is a surprisingly orderly crew. Expecting a group of grizzled pirates, what I find upon entering the Gifted Minds building instead is a detailed, incredibly well-lubricated machine.

Despite the ash-coated outdoors, the interior is immaculate. The furnishings are plain, but each workstation is orderly, papers and devices neatly arranged. Despite the dozens of scientists working in the front lobby, the noise level never rises above a library whisper.

Whatever Matt left here, these people clearly believe it's the key to their survival. That means at least some of our ideals should be aligned.

Reno, Evelyn and I turn down a wide hallway. I realize that the building's flat construction was not accidental—it was a design feature to make the program feel less like a strange governmental operation and more similar to a child's natural schooling experience. Aside from ripping the children away from their parents, the Circle didn't do a bad job in making the transition normal. The rows of lockers and faded corkboards remind me of my own misspent youth.

"Come in here for a moment," Reno says. Evelyn and I follow him into a classroom where the desks have been cleared out. A series of illegible steps are scribbled on the chalkboard. The pinkish floors are buffed to a shine, reflecting the flickering fluorescent lights. Two lab technicians in long white coats confer at the room's center. They stand at attention when they see Reno.

"Sir—we didn't know you were visiting today, sir."

"At ease, gentleman," Reno says. "I got a couple of people you need to meet."

"Sir?" The head technician is clearly uneasy. I realize it's because we look *rough*. It's been weeks since we've bathed. Our clothes are a patchwork of mismatched tatters. Certainly warm, but hardly winning any fashion awards. For the first time, I'm aware of the itchy growth on my face. It's a more welcome annoyance than seeing Ramses all the time.

"This is Luke Stokes," Reno says. Both men's jaws drop. "And this is his lovely friend, Evelyn…I'm sorry, I don't know your last name."

I'm amused at how proper and statesmanlike he is in their presence. With us, it's like he's shooting the shit over some pool.

"Vera," Evelyn says.

"Yes, Evelyn Vera." Reno takes off his hat and pats his bald head. "From what I've gathered, these folks know quite a lot about HIVE. Been a part of it, in fact."

The head technician has to push up his glasses. Probably wondering if he's hallucinating this entire encounter. Then he says, in a much more serious voice than I'd like, "If they've been inside…"

"Yes, the documents we have indicate that's problematic." Reno pauses, then puts his hat back on. "But I trust you boys can sort it out."

"Yes, sir. We will, sir. Thank you, sir."

Reno walks toward the door.

"The hell you going?" I say. Behind me, I can almost *feel* the shock of the two technicians. Not that I care. I'll talk to him however I damn well please, because it's apparent he needs me. Until he doesn't. Then Reno will be like all the rest.

"We've read extensively about the hallucinations," Reno says. Before he closes the classroom door, he adds, "Consider it a show of our good faith."

The hinges creak, leaving us alone with the two techs. They almost seem afraid to approach us. Maybe they're terrified that my insubordination will rub off.

But then the head tech says, "Before we begin, I believe a shower is prudent. The instruments, you see…they are quite sensitive."

I turn to Evelyn and grin. "I think he's saying you smell like shit."

She flushes slightly and rolls her eyes. "One day, that's gonna get you in trouble, Luke."

"What is," I say as we follow the tech toward the back of the room, where a door links to a repurposed scrubbing station.

"You're gonna snake charm the wrong person," she says, her eyes deadly serious. "And you're gonna get bitten."

What concerns me most is that she thinks we haven't already been bitten pretty damn badly.

*

TURNS OUT THE technicians' worried looks were for nothing. It's a quirk of the scientist to wonder whether your results and theories will pass muster in the field of reality. The con man, he runs on pure illusion and confidence. It's right in the name, after all. These eggheads have been poring over Matt's files for the better part of a year. Whatever fix he'd developed for some of his purposely designed HIVE glitches must've been in there somewhere.

It's almost strange—when I blink, no images greet me. They've become such familiar companions that it's almost like losing a friend.

"All done," the head tech says. "Your readings are clear."

He's been testing me for the past hour. It's well past midnight. Next to me, his partner has been doing the same to Evelyn, despite her repeated protests that she was never really messed up to begin with.

The head tech looks surprised that I'm actually okay. He rubs his glasses on his lab coat and goes over the readings again.

"Oh my—what's *that*," I say, pointing to the blackboard. "It's *alive*."

A panicked look spreads across his face as he begins recalibrating the machine. "I must've missed a figure. The coefficients might be incorrect. I can't believe—"

I hop off the padded exam table and give him a wink. "I'm just messing with you, Doc."

He blinks. "I'm not a doctor." The other part of my statement doesn't seem to register.

"So, tell me," I say. "What does the boss man want with HIVE, anyway?"

The past few years have taught me to be suspicious of anyone intensely interested in HIVE's capabilities. The head tech sputters and haws, going on about how he's not authorized to talk about confidential information.

"Let me tell you something," I say, when he's done chasing his tail, "I've been seeing this place for *months*." I step closer, so only a half foot separates us. He's a bigger man, but he hasn't endured the same hardships. "Least I deserve to know is why you need me."

He clears his throat and diverts his gaze, looking to his assistant for help. The other man suddenly becomes very interested in the pink floor tile, as if it holds the secrets to life.

The head tech finally says, "You'll have to ask Commander Reno."

I whistle, like I'm impressed. "Commander." I nod toward Evelyn, who's getting off the table. "You hear that, Ev? A *commander*."

"A real, honest-to-God commander? Wowee."

I shoot her a glance. "Too much."

"Really?" She wrinkles her nose. "Oh well."

The two technicians look confused, like they've entered a weird alternate social reality that they just can't possibly understand.

"Look," I say, placing my arm around the head tech's neck like we're old pals, "I just need to know what you guys have planned."

"I really can't tell you, Mr. Stokes."

"Then I really can't help you," I say, my arm sliding slowly away to illustrate how tenuous this alliance can be. "Sorry."

I wink at Evelyn, and we start walking toward the door.

"W-wait," the head tech says, unable to grapple with the idea that he could scuttle my involvement. "There's a—I think it's a program. A piece of software."

"I'm listening," I say.

"It's a kill switch," the head tech says. "Shuts the entire thing down. Or…maybe kill switch isn't the correct term."

"I don't need the technical specs. That'll do."

"N-no, that's not what I meant. Because I think the fail-safe can also…hand off control."

I lean against the doorway and act like this information is boring. "What's the big deal?"

"It hands off control to HIVE," the head tech says. "The system will make its own decisions."

"Interesting."

I walk away, Evelyn hurrying behind me.

"Interesting," she says when she finally catches up. "That's all you have to say?"

"Guess we got a big decision to make."

"And what's that?"

"I'll let you know when I know."

26 | SALVO

WE CATCH A nap in the common area, curled up together on a luxurious coach. In the morning, we're woken by one of the Oshies, who leads us to a doorway that has ADMINISTRATOR'S OFFICE etched on the glass.

The Oshie knocks, and Reno says, "Come in."

Evelyn and I do as we're told and shut the door behind us. The room is unspectacular, overflowing with papers and files.

"Love what you've done with the place," I say.

"It's not much," Reno says. "A mansion compared to the ship." He motions for us to sit down on the worn folding chairs.

"How'd you guys even find the institute?" I glance around the room for clues. Hard to tell how anyone can even think in this mess. But apparently this is where Reno—*Commander* Reno—runs operations from. "It's kind of—I don't believe in luck."

Reno has his bare feet propped up on the plain beige desk. He strokes his shiny head while I speak, nodding along. It's a good gesture. He's trying to build my trust. Must work gangbusters on the rest of these idiots.

Me, I've been burned a couple times too many. Although I am thankful that a hundred-pound imaginary dog is no longer following me around all the damn time. It's funny, because the way I remember it, Ramses was all right inside HIVE. Don't know why my subconscious turned him into such a raging dickbag in reality.

That's one for the shrinks to sort out when this mess is over.

"Good, 'cause I don't believe in luck, either." Reno sips from a whiskey tumbler. "We picked up a long-range radio frequency transmission. Morse Code." He pours himself another drink. Evelyn and I have only been in the tight office for five minutes, and he's already knocked back three fingers of whiskey. "I tell you, your brother was some kind of genius."

"Thanks for letting me know." There's a wall full of degrees hanging behind Reno's chair. They don't belong to him, but I find it amusing that he doesn't care enough to clear them out.

"Y'all having side effects?" He wipes liquor from his wispy mustache, waiting patiently for a response.

"All good." I grit my teeth, then I say, not entirely meaning it, "Thanks for that."

"Thanks for bein' our guinea pigs."

"The pleasure's all ours, I assure you," I say. "So you pick up this radio signal offshore."

"Radio ain't real common these days, with all the fancier stuff working its magic in space. I guess we were the first to hear it." Reno shrugs with an *aw shucks* expression. "Or maybe just the first fool enough to believe it."

"Hope's a dangerous mistress."

"That she is," Reno says. "But we came in from the

shore and we used a lotta what your brother wrote to make this place semi-habitable. This place is incredible. The work they did, in just a few months, that young."

"Few months?"

"They shut it down quick," Reno says. "You can read the official records, you want." He gestures toward a stack of tall files in the corner. "They're all real interesting."

"I'll pass," I say. "Tell me about where I enter this equation."

Evelyn snorts lightly. Yeah, yeah, it's always about me.

"You only gotta read one thing to find that out," Reno says. "You up for that?"

"Depends on how long it is," I say.

"Never tip your hand and agree to a promise you can't keep. I like that."

Reno reaches into the bottom drawer of the desk. With a certain care, he extracts a single sheet of paper. He holds it out, over the messy surface.

I take it from him and skim it. In so many words, it's the basic outline of HIVE's capabilities. Matt must've left it here, along with the fail-safe code. Most of it I already know: HIVE stands for HoloBand Interactive Virtual Existence. His shadow plan was to broker peace, after Chancellor Tanner commissioned the program. If, for some reason, HIVE fell into the wrong hands—well, he had a fail-safe hidden in a locker here, where his journey began.

Only the last line is relevant to me. It completes the memory fragment I saw at Atlas' way station.

If the wrong person gets HIVE, a good man will know what to do. Luke Stokes will know what to do.

I look up when I'm finished. Reno's been eying me this whole time, trying to gauge my reaction. Before I speak, I hand Evelyn the paper.

"So, y'all see what's going on. Why I was so excited to find you, Luke."

"Not really," I say.

"You don't know what to do?" He raises a graying eyebrow. His wind-beaten skin scrunches up around the corners of his eyes. "Well then, why'd I bring you here?"

Evelyn breathes quicker. I don't. I look right through Reno and say with lackadaisical ease, "I know what to do." I reach into my back pocket, taking the worn and frayed printout Atlas gave me. That meeting feels like years ago. With methodical slowness, I unfold it and offer it to Reno.

"I can't read this," Reno says. "You can?"

"Your nerds can," I say. "That's why you pay them the big bucks, right?"

"If you can't read it, you don't really know."

I direct my gaze at him, so white-hot that he has to look away. "Call it faith, right?"

A man can't argue with his own words. He nods.

"I'll take you to your brother's work."

He rises and slips past us. As he's working the fickle doorknob, the building shakes and dust comes down from the ceiling.

"What's that?" I say.

"Sounds like a—"

Turns out it's just the opening salvo.

Because then the office wall crumbles in a smoky explosion, sending me to the floor.

27 | ROULETTE

"GODDAMNIT," RENO YELLS above the smoke and noise. "The hell happened out there?"

I wriggle out from beneath him. "Evelyn? Evelyn?" My voice rises in pitch, frantic, hopeful—dreading that no answer will come. Eyes stinging from the smoke and dust, I push through the swirling heat and bitter cold, fingers searching. They brush against something soft. It smells ever so faintly of lilac.

"I—I'm stuck."

The words fill my chest with ice and elation simultaneously. "Can you move?"

"The files are…" She grunts, a labored breath expelled from her lungs. "They're on top of me."

I move my hands further along, catching the crinkled edges of manila folders and dense stacks of paper. This doesn't seem so bad. My hands move down, and hit metal. Heart dropping, I press against the cabinet.

Evelyn whimpers softly like a wounded animal when I try to move it.

"It hurts, Luke."

My reply is devoured by another explosion. The office's light fixture crashes down and explodes in a shower of sparks two feet from my head. Reno curses, apparently nicked by some of the debris. Flames lap at the massive hole in the office wall. Through the roiling smoke, I spot the ruined flagpole. I could walk out of here.

But that would mean I have to leave Evelyn behind.

"Help me, Reno," I yell through the blurry room. My free hand swings about, brushing past his slick head. "She's beneath the cabinet."

"We gotta get the damn fail-safe," Reno says. "It's underground. Bastards are coming for it."

"She stays, I stay."

"You have to leave, Luke," Evelyn says as another shell explodes twenty feet away. The building shakes, ash sent whirling into the air again. The smoke parts for a brief moment as an arctic breeze whips through. In the chasm in the wall, I see troops advancing methodically. They're still outside the institute's gates. If they ran fast, they could be here within half a minute. But I suspect the fight with the Oshies has been a bloody one, and they're wary of tricks.

A sniper shot cracks out, and the invaders immediately drop to the ground. Then the debris cloud forms again, leaving me unable to even see the tiny office's ruined walls.

"*Reno.*"

"All right, lead me to y'all."

I grab the thick padding of his jacket and guide him toward Evelyn. When I place his hand on the cabinet, I say, "You push on my command."

"Don't do it," Evelyn says, panicked. "Just leave me."

I ignore her and say, "Now."

We push, the cabinet's heavy groan not nearly loud enough to drown out her screams. Outside, Kid Vegas' army trades shots with the Oshie soldiers defending the institute. I have no way of telling who's winning the battle. But if the attack is enough to crack through Reno's cowboy cool, then it has me worried.

I lift Evelyn to her feet. She leans against me, putting all her weight on one leg. "Compound fracture," she says underneath her breath. "Potential ligament damage. Kneecap dislocation probable…"

As we turn around, looking for the door, she continues reciting her diagnosis. I don't say anything. It's taking her mind off the pain.

Reno yanks my arm toward the doorway.

"It's in the basement," he says.

Explosions buffet the building as we move through the halls. Here, too, the dust is thick, ceiling tiles and plaster hanging at precarious angles. Once we're a few feet into the halls, visibility increases enough that I can actually see in front of me. Not far, but enough.

Evelyn stumbles across a ruined locker, breaking her string of concentration. When she falls, I glimpse her leg and have to turn away. The bone is sticking through the back of her calf, crushed through the skin by the cabinet's weight.

I lift her off the ground and put her over my shoulder. Far down the hallway, the building shakes—this time from the lockstep footsteps coming up behind us.

"A good woman's hard to find," Reno says. He looks funny without the hat, his blue eyes shining through the gritty dust. A broken water fountain spits a small geyser into the air, spraying his head with a light film of moisture.

"You have no idea." I feel Evelyn sigh as I move.

"That Kid Vegas fella ain't gonna stop," Reno says. "Made that clear when he first came."

"You met him?" I adjust the weight on my shoulders so Evelyn's hip isn't digging into my joint.

"Met a man who knows the man," Reno says. "Let's just leave it at that." He nods toward an open doorway. In the low light dust, it's hard to tell what he's gesturing toward. When I get closer, I spot a stairwell. The building quakes again. It gives me the slightest idea what it must've been like when the fault line ruptured. The emergency lights leading to the basement tremble and sway.

"Or you could tell me."

Reno stops on the middle of the steps. "Y'all want to wait for story time?"

"The short version will do." No matter what position I arrange Evelyn in, each step feels like a pile driver going through my shoulder. I follow him down to the unlit basement. Scrounging around in the dirt, Reno eventually finds a tiny battery powered lantern. It casts a ghostly glow that barely cuts five feet ahead.

"He sent one of our captured boys back with a message." Dirt and rocks dislodge from the low ceiling. It's wide enough not to be claustrophobic. I still have to crouch slightly so that Evelyn's back doesn't hit the top. You wouldn't want to be caught down here for an extended period of time.

"What was the message?"

"Message was, half the boy's face was damn burned off," Reno says. "Implication bein', if we didn't give up, we were going to suffer."

Kid doesn't do cruelty for no reason. There's always a motive behind his actions—a motive, even, behind the motive. That's the thing with the people trained in Gifted Minds. They're a half dozen steps ahead, playing on a different game board.

Just like this frontal assault on the institute—it was a move Reno didn't anticipate. But what comes next, the chess move twenty minutes down the line, that's what I'm curious about. Kid Vegas and Olivia Redmond played me for a fool once before. Led me exactly where I needed to go, then they cherry-picked the fruits of my futile labor.

"What was your response?"

"The hell you mean, my response," Reno says.

"I mean, what'd you do? Your operation change at all?"

He stops in the tunnel, and I almost bump into him. "You questionin' my judgement?"

"Kid's got an end game in mind," I say. "I'm just trying to figure that out."

"Ain't too hard to figure out." Reno starts walking again, wiping his sweaty brow. That is a funny thing about being down here. The confined space traps our body heat, making it seem warmer than it actually is. "You best watch your head. And your girlfriend's leg."

I see why in another thirty paces. The tunnel narrows, the ceiling dipping to around four feet high. Reno ducks through the opening.

"This is gonna hurt, Ev," I say.

She groans, only half-awake. As gently as I can, I dip her so that I'm cradling her body in my arms. Then I crouch, hunched at the back, and hand her off through the hole. Reno grabs her, but the slight impact of the hand off makes her scream.

The noise echoes off the long tunnel as I squeeze through the entranceway.

He lays her down in a corner of the room. Her eyes are shut tight, trying to stave off the tears.

"My brother dig this tunnel?" I say, looking around. "This what you meant by his work?"

"We dug it out over the past year," Reno says. "Pain in the ass."

"Why bother?" The unfinished dirt room is about 9 x 9. The lantern isn't powerful enough to illuminate the whole thing. Instead of answering, Reno walks over to the corner and shines the light. A rickety ladder leads up-wards.

"In case of emergency," Reno says. "An escape tun-nel."

The pieces click together. "You responded with force, didn't you? When Kid sent you that soldier back with half his face missing."

"Can't let a man push you around," Reno says. "Shows weakness. You face the storm."

"So most of your forces are elsewhere?"

"We ain't got time for this," Reno says, heading to-ward a table where a small, ancient drive sits. Without even reading the label, I can tell that it's got something to do with HIVE. The technology is ancient—a 2.5" solid state drive. Only Matt could use something so old to cre-ate something so brilliant.

Then again, there's an old saying from great artists. It's the constraints that make innovation possible. So maybe, by zagging and pulling from the past, he was able to see a path that others couldn't. Not like I can ask him.

"This was what's in the locker," Reno says. "I assume you know what to do with it?"

"If you didn't lose the paper I gave you, then you'll know."

"Just checkin' to see if you had a change of heart." He pockets the drive and points at the ladder. "Shall we?"

"I don't think so."

His radiant blue eyes narrow. It's the first time I've seen him angry. "The hell you mean?"

"You sent your forces out for revenge," I say. "The majority of them, at least. Problem is, that did two things. One, you're gonna lose the media war. Their propagandists get to paint you as savage. Obliterating some small, overmatched force."

"That ain't the truth."

"Truth doesn't play into it," I say. "So Kid has the citizens of the NAS behind the military action. That's the first step. But the main thing is, he pushed you out of position. Opened you up to an attack."

Reno doesn't say anything. It's fifty-fifty whether the calm returns, or his anger boils over into a full blown storm. For the Oshies' sake, I hope it's the former. Being pissed off will get everyone killed.

"Let's say you're right," Reno says, his tone measured. "And I ain't sayin' you are. Then what?"

"Simple," I say. "He makes you panic. You're left unguarded. Probably think he has a bigger force than he does."

"A lot more than we got," Reno says, still guarded. Unwilling to let go of his notion that we have to rush through to the surface, haul ass away from the institute.

"That may be true at some point," I say. "But right now, you probably outnumber Kid's forces. I'd bet on it."

"You a roulette playin' man, Luke?"

"I prefer being the house," I say, holding his gaze. "Think about it. You pop out this hole, and you bring him

exactly what he wants, but hasn't found yet. The fail-safe."
I work backwards, how Kid could've gotten the intel.
"They must've found out about the fail-safe from Atlas."

"Atlas?" I'm throwing too much at Reno at once.

"Don't worry about it," I say. "Old friend. But, I
suspect, a dead one." Unless it was Jana, since she was
the only other person who really knew. But something
tells me she isn't dead yet. "Anyway, it's easier for Kid to
smoke you out than for him to fight a war of attrition."

"How you figure?"

"Because that's why the Circle isn't fighting the factions any more." It's all obvious now. Each move slots
in easily. Chancellor Blackstone is a smart man, far more
intelligent than his predecessor Tanner. It's easier to win
by guile than outright force. To *enlist* rather than *enforce*.

Any good grifter knows that. Without the mark's own
inertia, running a con would be a Sisyphean failure.

Right now, Blackstone is very interested in rebuilding.
Which doesn't sound bad, until you consider his methods.
To kill people while they're still living. That's what HIVE
is—what living in the New Allied States will be like. The
experience of being soul-crushingly dead while being
conscious for all of it. The worst kind of hell.

Maybe it takes people a couple years to realize. Like
what they exchanged before, in the Circle: stability for
their freedom. But when the quake hit and ash covered
the West, that civilization crumbled. And so will this false
front Blackstone and the others are erecting.

I consider all this and decide on a way forward. And
I must convince Reno of what I know, deep in my bones,
to be true. Blackstone taught Kid everything.

Which means that the move we're about to make—
the safe one—is the wrong one.

"I bet that man he sent back, he had his tongue cut out?"

Reno gives me a strange look. "How'd you know?"

"Because he probably told Kid about your little tunnel. Maybe just a rumor he heard after a few beers. But enough that Kid put the pieces together." I have a smug look of satisfaction. It's refreshing, to be neck-and-neck with genius. And oh-so-sweet to stifle a revenge attempt. "You pop out, I guarantee someone's up there waiting for us."

"A lot of moving parts," Reno says. But the skepticism has left his eyes. He's knows I've tangled with this particular beast before. Emerged with a couple deep cuts, but no mortal wounds. That experience can't be taught. Like surviving a giant swell in the middle of the sea. You count your blessings, batten down the hatches and make sure you don't run into the buzz saw again.

"You wanna hear what I got in mind?"

"Long as I tell my people it came from me," Reno says. "That's the deal."

It's not a power grab, but a plea for stability. "Tell them what you want. I got no dog in this fight."

"You got one," Evelyn says in a muted whisper.

"And what's that?"

"Me."

"Lady's got a point," Reno says. He steps away from the ladder and shakes my hand. "You may just be full of shit enough to survive."

I don't know if that makes sense, but I get what he's saying all the same.

28 | BUCKLE DOWN

THE GIFTED MINDS Research Institute is pockmarked by gunfire, its halls blackened by stray grenades and missiles. But the din of battle has already receded to a more distant front.

A soldier runs past a cluster of ruined lockers and stands at attention. "Commander. We've rebuffed the enemy forces."

Reno gives me a look and then says, "Gather the officers."

"Sir?"

"I have a special announcement," Reno says. "Set it for an hour. Tell them it's time to buckle down."

The soldier's eyes grow wide. "Yes, sir."

Then he darts away, running faster than before, buoyed by the very important message he now carries. I shift Evelyn's body on my shoulder, and she mumbles.

"What?"

"You need to put me down," she says. Her long blonde hair tickles my nose. I can't do anything about it, though, because balancing her now requires both of my arms. Every muscle around my neck burns, but I still keep walking. "You can't keep carrying me."

"Just be quiet."

"Carina's not your fault," she says. "I'm not your fault."

"You got kinda pissed when I told you that."

"Because you can be a condescending prick."

I laugh, and immediately regret it when her weight shifts slightly. She's right. If I'm going to help Reno and the Oshies, I can't be carrying her on my back the whole time. I'll just have to trust that she'll be okay.

A thin man runs toward us. His gaunt skin and unkempt hair make it clear that it's Martin.

"You're alive," he says. "Martin is very pleased." I notice that he has a guitar on his back. He catches me staring and says with a wide smile, "Martin found it in one of the rooms." It's an expression not driven by extrinsic motivations like women or wine or fame, but genuine passion.

Against my better judgment, I begrudgingly admit that this is slightly inspiring. Like the tiniest four-leaf clover growing on a massive mountain of shit. But it's a start.

His face falls when he realizes that Evelyn is hurt. "Is she…"

"I'm not dead, asshole," Evelyn says.

"Martin is pleased," he says, brushing his ratty hair out of his dirty face. "I'm pleased."

"Great," I say. "Do me a favor, would you?"

His face lights up. "I'll write a song about you."

Reno, who has been watching this exchange with a pleasant detachment, finally steps in and says, "Look, sir, Mr. Stokes is important. We have plans."

Martin gives him a funny look. "Mr. Stokes? This guy?"

"Martin," I say. "Just look after Evelyn. Get someone to set her leg."

"No songs," Evelyn says beneath her breath.

"Lots of songs," Martin says. "I have so many *ideas*, you know? Just tons of them. When the world comes back, maybe I'll go solo. Martin would be amazing solo. The other guys are probably dead, you know, which is a bummer—"

"*Martin*," I say.

"Right, right." He runs off before returning two minutes later with no less than half a dozen people. I hand Evelyn off, give her a wordless goodbye pat, and watch as they take her away.

Reno and I walk through the ruined institute. We stop in front of his office, but don't go inside. Just look through the doorway, at the huge hole in the wall.

"I hope you know what you're doin'."

"So far so good," I say. But his words send an icy fear through my chest. Maybe this is what Kid wanted all along.

But there's one wild card that gives me confidence.

Kid has no way of knowing I'm already here.

And the snake hiding in the brush is even more dangerous than the one you can't recognize.

29 | THE PLAN

ALL THE OFFICIALS and important military personnel gather in the institute's auditorium right before nightfall. It's a group of about thirty people, mostly men, although a couple tough looking women are present, too. They remind me of Jana. If I had to grapple with anyone, I'd prefer to take the burliest guy here. The more difficult the fight to the top, the tougher the animal. Grit has an interesting way of evening things out.

Reno stands at the lectern. A new cowboy hat, identical to the old one lost in the salvo, sits atop his head. He looks remarkably clean and put together. Fresh pressed jeans and a sport jacket, like he's ready for a date at a nice steakhouse.

Each faction's customs amuse me, since I have none of my own. I think that's true atheism—having no superstitions, no illusions about certain things. Always being prepared to use the right tool for the right task. Maybe I'm just fooling myself and can't see my own beliefs. That tends to be how it is. After all, didn't I lap that shit up about being a hero, on some level?

Reno taps the microphone. The buzz in the auditorium abates as everyone settles into the vinyl seats. It's a fairly large place, easily seating three hundred. Most of the chairs are empty, showing just how much humanity hangs by a thread. And here we are, talking about how we'll kill more of us.

Before starting, Reno walks over to share a word with me on the side of the stage, where I'm leaning up against a giant projection screen that reminds me of the tent city in the Black Hole. The one that shattered in two and almost crushed me.

"You cool with me taking all the credit, right?"

"Nervousness doesn't look good on you, Reno." I don't say it, but I liked him better when he wasn't afraid to die out by the Pacific Lodge. But he hasn't known me for very long. There's still a doubt in his mind—maybe going up the ladder was the right call. We could be sitting ducks here. Kid Vegas could still be another step ahead.

I see all this in his eyes.

"I'm goin' all in with you," Reno says. "You know how that feels, don't you?"

I look out at the expectant audience. The Oshies are placing their faith in their commander—that he has answers which they cannot see. I'm uncomfortable with deification, but in this case, I do know things they do not. For I have been in Kid's jaws, and I have survived.

Not without paying my pound of flesh, of course. Matt is gone. HIVE threatens to turn everyone into passive floating heads. Carina died. Three years have vanished. Evelyn is injured. And one of my closest allies is a junkie ex-rock star who tried to rob me.

So yeah, I know about going all in. I'm learning more about faith than I want to know. It's not comfortable for me, either, since I've always been the one exploiting others' tendencies to believe.

"That's why you're following my plan," I say.

Reno holds my gaze for a moment, then walks back to the lectern.

He begins addressing the audience. Official and polite. They hang on every word. After he outlines the plan, it takes a moment for the implications to sink in. I glance across the stunned room, half-expecting someone to burst out, scream that it's lunacy.

But the Oshies are nothing if not loyal. Surviving the unpredictable seas has made them trust those above them. There is no time for second-guessing when the waves are churning, threatening to blast apart a platform. You simply must have faith that your superiors have done their due diligence while you were battening down the hatches.

Everyone rises wordlessly a minute later and files out of the auditorium.

"They might hate me forever, this don't work," Reno says. A sizable chunk of tobacco and put it in his cheek. Gives a round sound to his words. He spits on the floor. A year of taking care of this place and none of it will matter in a few hours.

"Evelyn's out of harm's way, right," I say.

"You got our map," Reno says, staring out at the empty room for what will be the last time. "You seen our operation. It's a little bigger, now. Get new ships coming in every coupla weeks."

"You still got people out on the seas? Shit."

"Some of 'em prefer it," Reno says. "A man can get used to anything."

He spits again and walks across the stage, his boots ringing out on the thin wood.

"I need the chopper here in thirty minutes."

"It'll be ready in twenty," Reno says, pausing in the doorway. "My boys won't let you down."

As he disappears and the door clicks shut, I hope silently that I'll hold up my end of the bargain.

And that my plan is right.

30 | THE REVERSE CON

ONCE YOU GAIN a reputation for the grift, it's rare that people try to fleece you. Sure, you get some loose cannons who try to match wits. We always cleaned those idiots out. But occasionally someone good would slide through town. These guys were always dangerous—get too close, and you'd get burned, just like anyone else. The temptation, though, to improve your skills, stake out your territory, it was hard to resist.

Hence the reverse con. Where someone's tagged you as a mark—but, really, they're the mark.

Someone like Kid Vegas, though, you're not playing with fire with a plan like mine. You're toying with a kind of pain that you're not even sure exists. All I know, is if this doesn't go off, I'll find out what he's got in store. And it'll be nastier than before.

The chopper's rotors blow back my hair as it touches down in the road. After a couple seconds, the pilot manages to settle onto the chewed up ground. The terrain looks worse than when I came in, and it didn't look great to begin with. Kid's bluff was a damn good one—a bark with just enough bite.

I hurry to the chopper.

"You Luke?" The pilot's an old-timer, the kind with more vitality than an eighteen-year-old.

"Yeah."

"Benny," he says. "Climb in." When he offers a hand to pull me up, his grip is shockingly strong. He notes my expression and says, "From lashin' lines and hangin' on for dear life in the waves."

Then he laughs, long and rolling, as I close the door.

"Reno told you the plan," I say. "I'm presuming."

"Goin' straight into the heart of the enemy's camp," Benny says. "You got balls, kid. I like that."

The chopper lifts off, leaving the dust swept street and rubble behind. From above, the landscape looks like a child has left their toys a jumble. And that everything will be all right once his parents tell him to clean everything up.

But nature doesn't work that way.

The world doesn't work that way.

The buildings crushed on top of another like a pile of cracker crumbs will take many years to fix. Even getting back to whatever the North American Circle was, before it all fell down, will be a struggle.

The question, then, is simple: what path do we want to travel? At the end of those years, do we want to surpass our old existence, or just create a more resilient version of the machine we all hated?

My mind's already set. I'm in the chopper.

It's everyone else that I'm worried about.

"Where'd you get the bird," I say. "Doesn't strike me as too useful on the boat."

"It ain't," he says. "There was a warehouse full of 'em outside downtown Seattle. Can you imagine that? The roof was light enough, they survived gettin' buried."

"Lucky."

"Sometimes the world throws ya a bone after kicking your ass." Benny plays with the sound system. "Only music they had was kinda shit, though."

I listen to the opening bars. They sound familiar. "What's this?"

"Some shit by this Rhinoceros band," Benny says. "I don't know. My kid woulda liked 'em, I think. She had shit taste in music."

"I'm sorry," I say.

"For what?"

"Your kid."

He glances over, gives me a kinda shrug. "It is what it is, ya know? I'm still here." Not sure he sounds super happy about it. Another man's discontent can be a tricky thing to gauge. Maybe his tremendous energy is betraying him, and all he wants to do is die.

But Benny dispels that notion when he says, "It's all right. I figure, we get everything up and running again, she'd be proud." Then he nudges me with an elbow. "Besides, I got a couple young broads sitting around to take my mind off things."

"That helps," I say, not really listening. I'm examining a trail of smoke on the horizon. We've traveled about twenty miles northeast. Reno's scouts claim this is where Kid Vegas has set up his main base.

Until an hour ago, the Oshies were laying siege to it. But it's a pain in the ass fighting a battle when your opponent has state of the art drone defenses. Courtesy of Blackstone's stockpile, no doubt.

It's a razor's edge, what Kid is doing. But then, so is my response. We're both gambling, hoping that the roll doesn't come up snake eyes.

"They've been hittin' it pretty hard." Benny eases up on the throttle, to slow down as we enter less friendly airspace. "Reno was pretty adamant about that."

"I heard."

"He don't change his mind much," Benny says. "Must've seen something written in the stars."

"Something like that," I say. The dense smoke is an acrid shade of blackish gray. It streams from the walls around the settlement. Kid has only been here a few weeks, but it's a surprisingly sophisticated operation, given that time constraint. Must've had some of the Gifted Minds' nano-builder bots lying around to help him out.

It reminds me of the enemy I'm about to square off with: ruthless, focused and with far more resources. The Oshies are tough, but they're like a less-crazed version of the Remnants. Nomads struggling to survive and find a home.

That's why I'm so damn important. I can actually think like Kid, Blackstone, Olivia Redmond. Because I *am* them, on some level.

The trick is not to become them completely.

"I'm gonna swing down and around," Benny says. "The charge should go off in—yeah, there she goes."

Just like the plan, one of the walls erupts in a massive plume of flame. It belches horrid amounts of smoke into the air, blanketing the airspace. It's all for show—and cover. The chopper dips down lower and plunges straight into the gray.

"They'll know you're coming," Benny says. "No avoidin' that. But they won't know *when* or exactly *where*."

"That's what I'm counting on." I take the parachute from the backseat and adjust the straps. Test them to make sure they're secure.

"Anyone tell you this?" Benny says, navigating through the zero-visibility conditions with detached cool. I count the seconds in my head, using the speed gauge to calculate when I should jump. "You might be the craziest son of a gun I've ever seen."

"I'll take that as a compliment."

Then I open up the chopper door and jump, frigid wind streaming past my bare ears as I hurtle into the unknown.

31 | PLUSH DIGS

THE DRONES DON'T get me. The diversion has done the trick, sending enough smoke into the atmosphere to cloak my arrival. I hit the ground and roll, unclipping my chute as I pop up. The metal clips clang when they hit the hard ground. I cup my bare hands together and blow into them for warmth. There are many parts of this plan that resemble idiocy from the outside, but it's a particular brand of feigned ignorance.

Kid Vegas' scout base is surprisingly plush. The Remnants, if they co-opted this spread, would probably think it was the paradise of paradise. I'm in the housing district of the half-mile wide base. The buildings aren't densely packed, so there's little cover.

The smoke and ash still swirls in the air. I cough lightly. No respirator. Haven't worn one since I entered the Gray Desert, and I don't plan to start. Adopting the customs would be an easy excuse to stick around, stay awhile, get comfortable. Last time I did that, I spent three years with an imaginary dog.

I hear voices, so I ball up the parachute and run over to one of the pre-fab townhomes. With a smirk, I vault the plastic white picket fence and tumble behind an empty planter. I don't know what they're planning on grow-ing. Peeking out from my vantage point, I see two guards walking through the gritty swirl of dust in the streets. Their voices are slightly muffled by the *ksh-ksh* of their respirators.

"You saw the enemy chopper. We got orders," the first fella says.

"Man, it's so damn cold out here," the other guy says. "I don't care about any helicopters."

"Don't let Vegas hear you say that. Crazy son of a bitch. Burned a man's face half off."

"That was the enemy."

"Since when were these Oshies the enemy?"

"You're the one all about orders."

Their boots scrape past. I know they can't see me, but I hold my breath anyway. Then the bastards stop, and my heart pounds in my ears.

"I just hit something." The first guy sounds confused.

"It's a wasteland. You fling shit and you find more shit."

"No, it had a—*there*. You hear that?" He kicks around in the street, and I hear a metallic *ting*. I dig my fingernails into my palms to keep from screaming *fuck*. My brilliant plan, undone by a single, small clip.

"Probably a nail."

"Nah, man." I hear the guy drop to his hands and knees. "It's around here somewhere. Yeah, I got it." He's excited. I start to get up from the planter, searching for an exit. Visibility is too low to shoot them—and besides, the gun will give away my position. I'll be swarmed in seconds.

"It's just trash."

"No," the guy says. "It's a parachute clip. Someone dropped in around here."

"Lemme see." The other soldier grabs the object from his partner's gloved hand. Then he tosses it into the wastes. "Told you it was garbage. Drones would've shredded anyone who came through the airspace."

"Why'd you do that?"

"You're the one talking about Vegas burning a guy's face off. Imagine what he'd do to a guy that brings him a piece of trash. I'm helping, you man. We're like brothers. You're just the stupid one I gotta watch out for."

"Fuck you."

I stop listening to the rest of their conversation, relieved that my cover hasn't been blown by the smallest detail. When they're gone, I stand up and brush myself off. The dust has started settling from the explosion.

Then, behind me, I hear a familiar voice.

"It was a nice try, Stokes," Kid Vegas says, his tone making my blood chill into slushy ice, "but as always, you're one step behind."

A pistol hammer clicks when I take a step forward.

"It's been so long since we've had a chat," Kid says. "Going so soon?" The lonely wind rips past my ears. "Nothing to say? No clever replies? Color me disappointed."

But all I can think of is *the plan*.

In thirty minutes, there are people counting on me.

And if I don't deliver, they'll all die.

32 | GREAT SACRIFICE

"The drones may have missed you coming in, but I sure didn't," Kid says. "Although I wasn't expecting to see you."

"Surprise," I say. I don't answer or turn around. I still haven't looked at him. The longer that stays the case, the better.

"I was wondering why old Reno didn't take the bait," Kid says. "Reno always loses to Vegas, don't you think?"

"Not this time," I say.

"But then I see you, Stokes, and it makes sense. Once bitten, twice shy. Gotta say, I didn't expect you to get smarter in that little virtual world. But hey, even a blind dog finds a bone every now and again."

"People don't say that."

"You should know that by now, Stokes."

"Know what?"

"I'm not most people," Kid says, and real proud of it.

"Guess I won't feel bad about killing you, then."

"This is a nice knife," Kid says. He stripped me of any weapons I had with an annoying lackadaisicalness. Like I couldn't kill him even if I was strapped. "Sharp."

After a short walk, we reach what must be Kid's operational control room. On the one hand, I should be pleased. This is where I wanted to go all along. So, technically, the plan is right on schedule. On the other hand, I have a large problem—I can't exactly execute what I need to do with a gun pointed at my head.

"Blackstone gives you the best work," I say. "Vacation out west."

"I requested this assignment, Stokes," Kid says. "Door's open."

"You know there are thieves around," I say, mentally trying to calculate how much time has elapsed. Five minutes, maybe. "Not safe to leave your doors unlocked."

"I think I caught them all."

So he knows I don't have backup. The bluff was worth a shot.

The metal pulls at my skin when I grip the icy knob. I walk into the dim lit room. Dozens of workstations line the walls, all displaying different operational details.

No one else is present.

"All for you?" I say.

Kid doesn't turn on the light. Apparently the digital glow is enough for him. "I like to keep personally apprised of things. Why don't you sit?"

I do as I'm told, settling into a leather rolling chair that's shockingly comfortable. Kid walks past, gun still trained on me. It's the first actual look I've gotten at him. His expedition into the Gray Desert hasn't prematurely aged him.

His eyes glint as he rips off the respirator. The flashing multi-colored screens cast a strange glow over his pale skin. He stares down his sharp nose, like he's trying to figure out if I have another play in my pocket. I don't, but my mind is working furiously. Making a break for it and hoping he'll miss isn't an option. Kid's an excellent shot.

"What do they call people like you?" I say.

"Savants," Kid says. "I don't pay much attention."

"No, I got it," I say, watching him tweak a parameter at one of the workstations. "They call you an asshole."

"I'm hurt," Kid says, not turning around. The soft *tap-tap* of the keys is the only noise for the next few moments. "We were friends, once upon a time."

"That's a stretch."

"Depends on what you consider a friend," Kid says. "You could still be in HIVE, living the life, Stokes. Kind of silly to be playing around in this gray sandbox, don't you think?"

"Place just wasn't for me," I say. "You gave me a shitty dog."

Kid laughs. "We've worked out a lot of the bugs in your brother's programming. You know, we don't even need you any more."

"So why am I alive," I say. "You want the HIVE bounty?"

"Because I want to know what those Oceanic Coalition bastards are planning," Kid says. He sits down across from me, leaning his elbows on the long table. One of the workstations beeps in the background, but I warrant his full attention now. "I want that fail-safe the man told me about as I threatened his children. And you're who's going to tell me."

"What'd you do to Atlas?" I shiver, realizing that Jana's bloodthirstiness might've been warranted. He, I kind of figured he was dead, but I'd forgotten about the kids.

"Was that his name?"

"What'd you do to his family, you son of a bitch?" I rise from the chair. Kid shakes the gun at me like I've been naughty.

"The same I'm gonna do to you, if you don't tell me what I need to know."

I take a deep breath and then sit down. Emotions aren't going to fix this situation.

"You'd like that, wouldn't you?" I put my dirty boots up on the table and stretch out.

"See, I'm glad you're here." Kid taps the gun's stock against the table. It reminds me of the time, each tap a second burning off into the ether. "It didn't add up. I knew Reno was *rattled*. Shaken to his very core. All that dipping and *aw shucks* shit, it goes away when you turn the heat up high enough. It was a problem I couldn't solve, why he wasn't following my plan."

"Thanks for the psychology lesson," I say. "If I'd known you were giving classes, I would've come earlier." I kick dirt off my boots. This clearly bothers Kid, but he can't do much about it. Shooting me isn't much of an option when he still needs information. This is like a chest of gold bullion being airdropped into the center of his camp. You don't just light that on fire. Right now, we're on the carrot portion. Soon, we'll come to the stick.

I can't wait.

A little voice shouts in the back of my mind: *do something*. Over and over. But his pistol is still flatly pointed at my chest. I move too quick, he'll blow me away, take his chances that he can run another gambit on Reno.

If only he knew that the HIVE fail-safe source code was beneath my shirt. He missed it when he searched for weapons.

"Glad my appearance helped you put the pieces together," I say. "Your old buddy Luke Stokes, pissing in your cereal again."

"I recall that I caught *you* last time around."

"You're going to love what's coming next," I say. "Love it."

"I don't think so," Kid says. "What you don't understand—truly understand—is intelligence. The implications of mine, or—more importantly—HIVE. Your silly fail-safe, it really is quite ridiculous. No more than a mosquito-like nuisance."

"Must've been how Matt felt about you."

He bristles and says, "You couldn't possibly understand Gifted Minds."

"Duly noted," I say. "Maybe you should speak slower. Use smaller words."

"Aren't you curious how I found your landing spot, when the drones couldn't even see you?"

"Not really."

"I calculated the trajectory of your descent based on the chopper's entry angle and speed before you hit the smoke cloud," Kid says. "Human beings are quite predictable."

For some reason, I get the impression that he's using me as a proxy for Matt, who must've run circles around him. That would piss Kid off. He's calm and collected on the outside, but there's a reason he knew how to rattle Reno. He suffers from a similar weakness. Dig down, beneath the slight, strong form and all the skills, and there's a pain point.

"I'm sure my brother would've been impressed."

His sharp nose flares. "Your brother's dead. Unplugged. And I'm still standing."

"Not for long—do you have the time?" I say casually. "Matt's documents were *very* interesting. A whole plan for what to do in case HIVE became active. I'm just following instructions."

"You have a tell, Stokes. Bluffing ill-suits you."

"I don't think you've played enough poker with me to know that," I say. "But sure, I'm lying. Why not tell me the time?"

Kid glares at me and gets up. Checks one of the workstations and says, "It's an hour before midnight."

"The exact time," I say.

"11:04 PM," Kid says before reseating himself. He jabs the gun in my face. Losing it. A little further and I might be able to push him over the edge. "Matt wouldn't make a plan like this."

"No?"

"It's not his style," Kid says, with a satisfied smirk, temporarily regaining confidence, "no, he was far more subtle. You're an amateur playing amongst professionals."

"I didn't say we were gonna drop a bomb on you in thirteen minutes."

"Thirteen minutes?"

"Might be twelve, now," I say. "Better watch that clock." I keep cool, even knowing that the Oshies are totally fucked if I don't manage to get out of here soon. Their main base is gonna be gone for nothing and the ones sent to help me will die.

"You're full of shit."

"See, you want to know your problem, Kid?" I lean back in the chair, like I'm telling an old friend a fun story. "You didn't adjust for one thing."

"What's that?"

"Once bitten, twice shy," I say, using his own words

to drive the knife in deeper. The chair's wheels slam down as I come in closer. "Running the same gambit again on the same mark is a rookie move. You can't always expect others to do the heavy-lifting for you."

His teeth flash in a crooked smirk. "You're good, Stokes." He waves the pistols in a congenial way. "Very well done. You had me going. Get me riled up, lose my cool."

"Is it that transparent? I suppose it would be, for someone of your intelligence."

"Trivial," Kid says. "Whatever plan you were working on, it's done as long as you're dead."

He brings the pistol up to my head and clicks the hammer.

My heart beats faster and I swallow hard. Thoughts jump between a number of different scenarios, none of them particularly compelling.

I say, "You're right. You should shoot me."

"Don't try this childish bullshit on me, Stokes." But he doesn't shoot. "It's embarrassing."

"Because I don't understand this intelligence," I say. "You know what Matt really did?"

I can see that he desperately does, because his face is torn between pulling the trigger and asking. Finally, his curiosity gets the better of him. "What?"

Ego is a bitch. Even with Matt long gone, my brother is the gold standard—the benchmark everyone else in Gifted Minds compares themselves to. No wonder they killed him. It was as much about jealousy as it was about seizing control of work they could never do themselves.

I tear into the small opening with abandon. The truth

is most powerful when it's least expected. "He created a fail-safe, as you know. Your coders probably found little bits of it in the HIVE source. Maybe you corrected it."

"There were complications, early on."

"A lot of those were glitches," I say. "But one piece of code was a feature, meant for a single user to find. *Me*." I shrug and raise my eyebrow. "But you guys rolled up on Atlas, did your thing, right? So you know about that, too."

I stifle the wave of fury that washes over me.

Kid doesn't nod. His gelled side part moves slightly as the heater kicks on. But from the look in his lifeless eyes, this isn't what he's expecting. Then again, the pistol hasn't moved, so I can't consider it a victory yet.

"So yeah, Matt created a little code that would download into my mind if I was ever inserted into HIVE. Call it—what, you ever been on a scavenger hunt? No, probably not. They don't invite assholes on scavenger hunts."

His fingers scratch against the pistol stock "You got one minute to get to the point, Stokes. Before you join your brother."

"Right, that was personal, wasn't it? I'm sorry," I say with a fake smile. "Hit a nerve."

"The world's not gonna miss your bullshit. It's got enough of it already."

"I don't disagree," I say. "Here's the interesting part— the kicker, as they say. The part you don't know. What the fail-safe can do. Because I looked at the code."

"I know what a fail-safe is," Kid says with massive irritation. "It's in the damn word."

"That's where Matt outsmarted us both, yet again." I watch the pistol. It's quaking almost imperceptibly. Kid's anger is starting to override his intelligence. "But don't feel bad about it. After all, none of you created HIVE. Hell, you got kicked out before the HoloBands even became a thing, and that's like the tiniest gear in a massive—"

The dam breaks, and I watch as the pistol swings toward my jaw. I duck, and the butt clips the top of my hair. Kid squeezes the trigger, and my ears explode with a painful ringing. I slither across the table on my belly and reach for him.

He tries to get the pistol down again, firing another shot, but that one misses, too.

I see his mouth moving, but all I can hear is the endless ringing. But I like it better that way. The chair overturns, and his pistol bounces away. We both crash to the floor. My chin bounces off the scratchy carpeting.

It stuns me for a second, which is too long when you're fighting Kid Vegas. His hands are around my neck, and I can immediately feel the world going dark. Despite his small stature, he's incredibly strong.

I gasp and choke, trying to pry his fingers off. But it's like being caught by a robot. Nothing I do makes a difference.

So, instead, I try a different tack.

I let myself go limp, like my neck is broken and he's won. For a couple more seconds, he keeps pressing, then he lets up. Shakes me like a dog with a rabbit. Drops me to the floor.

"Piece of shit," he says with a snarl. I hear him lean back against the wall. He's panting heavily. I smile, my lips brushing the carpet. Whatever I dredged up, that shit was buried deep. Maybe it has something to do with his father, the infamous Damien Ford.

Must've never been good enough for daddy.

Should've seen that hot button earlier.

"I can't believe you made me do that, Stokes," he says with an eerie calm. "Maybe you were smarter than I thought."

His head hits against the wall as he continues to breathe hard and process the events. I crack one of my eyes, allowing me a glimpse of the workstation's wire rat-nest, the half-broken chair and Kid's pant leg to my left.

No sign of the gun.

And holding my breath is starting to become a problem.

"But I get the last laugh," Kid says. "Matt and Luke Stokes, both dead by my hand." He actually laughs at this, which almost me shiver, because it's not remotely funny. I guess it confirms that he pulled the plug on Matt's virtual consciousness. Whatever he's been through, Kid's been seriously warped.

I try the other eye, and find the pistol is beneath the table, only an arm's length away.

Now or never.

I inhale sharply and spring for the gun. The metal feels cold against my fingers. I remember theforged suicide note, how it spoke of great sacrifice.

Maybe this is what it means.

"You lying son of a bitch," Kid says, and grabs one of my legs, trying to claw his way up my body. I twist over and level the gun.

There's no time to aim.

I just fire.

33 | THE END OF THE BEGINNING

I HAVE THREE minutes to address the actual plan. I wipe blood off the workstation monitor and work the piece of code out of my pocket. The techs graciously copied his work over to a more technologically relevant medium. Probably the only reason Kid didn't find it—that bulky old 2.5" SSD would've been obvious.

The thin, bendable thumbnail-sized wafer merges with the upload pad when I place it on the surface. A window pops up on the screen, asking me to confirm that I want to send this data. I wave my hand in front to give my assent, and a little bar appears on screen.

The clock ticks over to 11:15 PM. Cutting it real close.

"No, no," I say as the upload pauses. "Come on." I try all the gestures I know, but it's demanding an authorization from Kid. Only problem is, he's dead, with a quarter of his jaw blown off. But it just wants a fingerprint. He's only been dead a few minutes. Maybe the system won't notice.

My knife is still in his pocket. I take it back, and close my eyes while I work off his index finger. Then I sprint back to the system and jab the bloody digit into the reader.

The bar disappears.

I hold my breath.

Success. Access authorized.

The satellite upload zips along—apparently the NAS' technology is far better than whatever was at the high-rise—and immediately installs the fail-safe code to HIVE's central server. A prompt comes up on screen as I check the time.

11:16 PM.

Lots of lives on the line, here. I told the Oshies that I would be finished with time to spare. Cutting it awfully damn close. But even with the crunch, I take a moment to consider what the system is asking me.

Shut down HIVE.

Or hand over the reins. Make the system sentient.

I recall the words from Atlas' hand: *you can't just pull the plug. The light of civilization will go out.* Matt's words, from the note left at the Gifted Minds Research Institute: *If the wrong person gets HIVE, a good man will know what to do. Luke Stokes will know what to do.*

An explosion outside brings my attention away from the screen. The bombing runs are starting. Every last drone the Oshies have. In case, I didn't make it. And to provide cover if I did.

If I don't get out of here, my rescue party is going to be toasted.

I think about the wasteland, all the terrible things I've seen. How bad the world has gotten.

And I make my decision. Not the one I told Reno I'd make. But the one I feel is best.

Then I run like hell out of the building. The smoke is already thick, and another bomb drops nearby. I gotta make it to the front gate, and I'm way more than a minute out. An ATV roars along the road, two soldiers responding to the threat.

"Hey," I yell, "Over here."

They look at me and slow down. Because of the swirling chaos, and the fact that I'm coming out of the operations center, they must think I'm Kid. They start driving toward me. Then I unload on them with Kid's pistol.

I'm not a great shot, but it does the trick. One guy falls off the ride, the other clings to the back of the vehicle. I rush over and kick him off. He's groaning from where I got him in the shoulder.

"It'll be over soon," I say. Then I grip the throttle as hard as I can and spin out. The explosions crescendo around me, starting from the east, just as we planned. I smile. It's nice to have someone listen to you for a change. But that satisfaction quickly turns into fear. The bombing runs are catching up with me, and there's no way to call them off.

Sometimes, fail-safes bites you in the ass.

Hopefully, this isn't one of those times.

I plead with the ATV to go faster. As the base crumbles behind me, I hear the engine growl and sputter, trying its best to respond. I begin putting some distance between the explosions and me.

But the gates ahead are closing. I hear gunfire, shouting. The NAS troops are engaging my rescue party. Muzzle flashes light up the guard towers.

I unload the last of my pistol's clip into the air, trying to draw their fire. Some of the guards turn their attention to me, bullets spattering the dusty asphalt. I swerve, trying to make myself hard to hit. Rifle shots glance off the ATV's hood. I huddle down, so that my head is level with the handlebars.

Ahead, the gates are open only a sliver. Maybe too tight to make it and definitely not enough runway to hit the brakes. I double down and squeeze my hand around the throttle so hard that I swear I dislocate a couple fingers.

An explosion erupts around the gate as I plunge through. The ATV's wheels wobble and whine from the heat and force as I rocket through the new hole. I ease off the throttle, realizing that the whole thing is about to disintegrate.

Last minute bursts of gunfire continue, until the rest of the base is devoured by the drones. I skitter off the ATV fifty yards outside the gate, tumbling into the dirt.

A man in a cowboy hat rushes over from the waiting helicopter.

"Well damn if you didn't do it," Reno says. "But we gonna die, you don't get up."

"What about the institute?"

"We blew it sky high, just like you said." Reno grabs my arm, and I will myself forward as the bombs continue to drop. Benny is already a couple inches off the ground as we climb in. "Got the footage ready to hijack their media with."

"Get ready boys," Benny says. The takeoff is violent and sudden, Benny whipping the chopper hard to escape the blast zone. Massive orange plumes are reflected by the bubble of the chopper's glass. The craft wiggles and spins as the dirt and smoke swirls around it.

A minute later, though, we emerge on the other side.

Reno breathes out and says, "Goddamn, you did it, Luke. You shut down that HIVE business."

That's when I drop the real bomb.

"I turned it on," I say. "It's alive."

"You're messin' with me."

"Just following instructions," I say. *Luke Stokes will know what to do.*

"What have you done?" Reno shakes me, but I ignore him, looking out at the ruined landscape. "I told my people to follow your plan, you son of a bitch."

Truth is, I have no idea what I've done. All I know is, something had to change.

A familiar voice comes on the satellite radio. Benny yells over the thrashing rotors, "I'm pickin' something up."

Reno lets go, and we both lean in to listen.

The voice is familiar, but computerized and artificial.

"Hello little brother," Matt says. "I figured you'd know what to do."

"Who the hell is this?" Reno says. "Vegas?"

"It's the voice of change," Matt says. "The keystone to a new world. I'll be in touch, Luke."

"Wait." But the radio bursts into static, and the console begins to spark. I stare at the wisps of smoke, wondering what I've done.

I took a leap of faith, and it might damn well kill us all.

Which begs the question.

Did I end everything, like Jana needed me to?

Or is this just the beginning?

END OF BOOK 2

If you enjoyed *Ruins of the Fall*, please leave a brief review on Amazon. Each one is a huge help. Thanks!

To receive an email when the final book in the Remnants Trilogy, *Remnants of the Fall*, is released, please sign-up for the free newsletter at nicholaserik.com/news.

NOVELS BY NICHOLAS ERIK

KIP KEENE ADVENTURES

A series of standalone adventure novels starring space pirate turned treasure hunter Kip Keene, who saves the world from threats both ancient and mythical with the help of his partner Samantha Strike. (sci-fi/adventure)

The Emerald Elephant (Book 1): after Kip Keene crash lands on Earth, he finds an old ally in pursuit of an ancient Incan artifact that can take them both home. If they leave, the Earth will be destroyed.

The Ruby Rattlesnake (Book 2): when a wounded genetically engineered soldier stumbles into Kip Keene's office with an encrypted thumb drive, he and Samantha Strike must trace the contents back to Atlantis - and a long-dormant weapon.

The Silver Songbird (Book 3): when a former ally turns on Kip Keene and tries to erase history, he and Samantha Strike must travel back to 19th century China in order to keep themselves - and the world - from being obliterated.

The Diamond Dragon (Book 4): after finding a leather journal from another dimension in the basement of his newly inherited mansion, Kip Keene must enter the portal to the mythical land of Shambhala before a 2,000-year-old prophecy is fulfilled.

The Jade Jaguar (Book 5): when Kip Keene's sister is kidnapped by an off-book government organization, he's blackmailed into finding the truth about Area 51 - but a familiar face wants whatever is in Roswell, too...

The Golden Gazelle (Book 6): Kip Keene travels to a lost Aztec city with ties to the Knights Templar in search of his greatest treasure yet - but when he and his companions are trapped within the ancient walls, he must find out a way to destroy the city and keep the artifact from a familiar foe's grasp.

The Kip Keene Box Set: Books 1, 2 & 3

The Kip Keene Box Set: Books 4, 5 & 6

THE REMNANTS TRILOGY

When the western territories of the North American Circle are buried in ash, con man Luke Stokes must navigate a dangerous factional landscape - a totalitarian regime, a church of true believers and a group of rebels - to survive what remains after the fall.

Ashes of the Fall (Book 1)

Ruins of the Fall (Book 2)

Remnants of the Fall (Book 3)

Remnants: The Complete Trilogy (Books 1, 2 & 3)

THE SHADOW CONSPIRACY TRILOGY

Private Investigators Kurt Desmond and Cassie Atwood find a 10,000-year-old cave painting hinting at the stunning inter-

stellar origins of civilization - while also warning of its immi-
nent destruction. (sci-fi/mystery/adventure)

Shadow Memories (Book 1)

Shadow Space (Book 2)

Shadow Sunset (Book 3)

The Complete Shadow Conspiracy Trilogy (Books 1, 2 & 3)

STANDALONE NOVELS

The Rapture: a man trapped in an endless time loop by his
former employer must break free to save the woman he loves.
(dystopian/time travel)

The Last Dreamer: when Devin Travis dreams, he enters the
minds of others - but when outside forces discover Devin's
ability, they will stop at nothing to use it for their own ends.

Vanishing Midnight: a century after the Earth's destruction, the
survivors live in sky cities rigidly separated by social caste - until Mathias Harris decides to escape the sky. (dystopian)

Paradise: a group of island vacationers desperately fight for
survival against the elements and each other when a viral out-
break cuts them off from the mainland. (post apocalyptic)

For exclusive updates & discounts on upcoming titles,
visit nicholaserik.com/news.

ABOUT THE AUTHOR

NICHOLAS ERIK IS the author of over a dozen science fiction and post apocalyptic novels. His series include the Remants of the Fall Trilogy, The Singularity Conspiracy Trilogy and six adventures featuring the enigmatic treasure hunter Kip Keene.

He currently lives on the East Coast.

To receive exclusive discounts, free books and news on upcoming titles delivered straight to your inbox, sign-up for his **free newsletter** at nicholaserik.com/news. There's zero spam and absolutely no BS.

www.ingramcontent.com/pod-product-compliance
Lightning Source LLC
Chambersburg PA
CBHW020321200626
46814CB00006BB/2346